Rebecca of Sunnybrook Farm

Shirley Temple EDITION

Rebecca of Sunnybrook Farm

by **KATE DOUGLAS WIGGIN**

*With illustrations from the motion picture
featuring* SHIRLEY TEMPLE

RANDOM HOUSE, NEW YORK

TO MY MOTHER

Library of Congress Catalog Card Number: 59-10877

CONTENTS

Her eyes as stars of Twilight fair;
Like Twilight's, too, her dusky hair;
But all things else about her drawn
From May-time and the cheerful Dawn;
A dancing Shape, an Image gay,
To haunt, to startle, and way-lay.

WORDSWORTH

Chapter One

"We Are Seven"

The old stage-coach was rumbling along the dusty road that runs from Maplewood to Riverboro. The day was as warm as midsummer, though it was only the middle of May, and Mr. Jeremiah Cobb was favoring the horses as much as possible, yet never losing sight of the fact that he carried the mail. His brimmed hat of worn felt was well pulled over his eyes, and he revolved a quid of tobacco in his left cheek.

There was one passenger in the coach—a small dark-haired person in a glossy buff calico dress. Whenever the wheels sank farther than usual into a rut, or jolted suddenly over a stone, she bounded involuntarily into the air, came down again, pushed back her funny little straw hat, and picked up or settled more firmly a small pink sunshade, which seemed to be her chief responsibility—unless we except a bead purse, into which she looked whenever the condition of the roads would permit, finding great apparent satisfaction in that its precious contents neither disappeared nor grew less. Mr. Cobb guessed nothing of these harassing details of travel. Indeed he had forgotten the very existence of this one unnoteworthy little passenger.

When he was about to leave the post-office in Maplewood that morning, a woman had alighted from a wagon, and coming up to him, inquired whether this were the Riverboro stage, and if he were Mr. Cobb. Being answered in the affirmative, she nodded to a child who was eagerly waiting for the answer. The child might have been ten or eleven years old perhaps, but she had an air of being small for her age. Her mother helped her into the stage-coach, deposited a bundle and a bouquet of lilacs beside her, superintended the "roping on" behind of an old hair trunk, and finally paid the fare, counting out the silver with great care.

"I want you should take her to my sisters' in Riverboro," she said. "Do you know Mirandy and Jane Sawyer? They live in the brick house."

Lord bless your soul, he knew 'em as well as if he'd made 'em!

"Well, she's going there, and they're expecting her. Will you keep an eye on her, please? Good-bye, Rebecca; try not to get into any mischief, and sit quiet, so you'll look neat an' nice when you get there. Don't be any trouble to Mr. Cobb."

"Good-bye, mother, don't worry; you know it isn't as if I hadn't traveled before."

The woman gave a short sardonic laugh and said in an explanatory way to Mr. Cobb, "She's been to Wareham and stayed overnight; that isn't much to be journey-proud of!"

"It *was traveling*, Mother," said the child eagerly and willfully. "It was leaving the farm, and putting up lunch in a basket, and a little riding and a little steam cars, and we carried our nightgowns."

"Don't tell the whole village about it, if we did," said the mother, interrupting the reminiscences of this experienced voyager. "Haven't I told you before," she whispered, in a last attempt at discipline, "that you shouldn't talk about nightgowns and stockings and—things like that, in a loud tone of voice, and especially when there's men-folks round?"

"I know, Mother, I know, and I won't. All I want to say is"—here Mr. Cobb gave a cluck, slapped the reins, and the horses started sedately on their daily task—"all I want to say is that it is a journey when"—the stage was really under way now and Rebecca had to put her head out of the window over the door in order to finish her sentence—"it *is* a journey when you carry a nightgown!"

The objectionable word, uttered in a high treble, floated back to the offended ears of Mrs. Randall, who watched the stage out of sight, gathered up her packages from the bench at the store door, and stepped into the wagon that had been standing at the hitching-post. As she turned the horse's head towards home she rose to her feet for a moment, and shading her eyes with her hand, looked at a cloud of dust in the dim distance.

"Mirandy'll have her hands full, I guess," she said to herself; "but I shouldn't wonder if it would be the making of Rebecca."

All this had been half an hour ago, and the sun, the heat, the dust, the contemplation of errands to be done in the great metropolis of Milltown, had lulled Mr. Cobb's never active mind into complete oblivion as to his promise of keeping an eye on Rebecca.

Suddenly he heard a small voice above the rattle and rumble of the wheels and the creaking of the harness. At first he thought it was a cricket, a tree toad, or a bird, but having determined the direction from which it came, he turned his head over his shoulder and saw a small shape hanging as far out of the window as safety would allow. A long black braid of hair swung with the motion of the coach; the child held her hat in one hand and with the other made ineffectual attempts to stab the driver with her microscopic sunshade.

"Please let me speak!" she called.

Mr. Cobb drew up the horses obediently.

"Does it cost any more to ride up there with you?" she asked. "It's so slippery and shiny down here, and the stage is so much too big for me, that I rattle round in it till I'm 'most black and blue. And the windows are so small I can only see pieces of things, and I've 'most broken my neck stretching round to find out whether my trunk has fallen off the back. It's my mother's trunk, and she's very choice of it."

Mr. Cobb waited until this flow of conversation, or more properly speaking this flood of criticism, had ceased, and then said jocularly:—

"You can come up if you want to; there ain't no extry charge to sit side o' me." Whereupon he helped her out, "boosted" her up to the front seat, and resumed his own place.

Rebecca sat down carefully, smoothing her dress under

her with painstaking precision, and putting her sunshade under its extended folds between the driver and herself. This done she pushed back her hat, pulled up her darned white cotton gloves, and said delightedly:—

"Oh! this is better! This is like traveling! I am a real passenger now, and down there I felt like our setting hen when we shut her up in a coop. I hope we have a long, long ways to go?"

"Oh! we've only just started on it," Mr. Cobb responded genially; "it's more'n two hours."

"Only two hours," she sighed. "That will be half-past one; mother will be at Cousin Ann's, the children at home will have had their dinner, and Hannah cleared all away. I have some lunch, because mother said it would be a bad beginning to get to the brick house hungry and have Aunt Mirandy have to get me something to eat the first thing.—It's a good growing day, isn't it?"

"It is, certain; too hot, 'most. Why don't you put up your parasol?"

She extended her dress still farther over the article in question as she said, "Oh, dear, no! I never put it up when the sun shines; pink fades awfully, you know, and I only carry it to meetin' cloudy Sundays; sometimes the sun comes out all of a sudden, and I have a dreadful time covering it up; it's the dearest thing in life to me, but it's an awful care."

At this moment the thought gradually permeated Mr. Jeremiah Cobb's slow-moving mind that the bird perched by his side was a bird of very different feather from those to which he was accustomed in his daily drives. He put the

whip back in its socket, took his first good look at the passenger, a look which she met with a grave, childlike stare of
friendly curiosity.

The buff calico was faded, but scrupulously clean, and
starched within an inch of its life. From the little standing
ruffle at the neck the child's slender throat rose very brown
and thin, and the head looked small to bear the weight of
dark hair that hung in a thick braid to her waist. Her face
was without color and sharp in outline. As to features, she
must have had the usual number, though Mr. Cobb's attention never proceeded so far as nose, forehead, or chin, being
caught on the way and held fast by the eyes. Rebecca's
eyes were like faith—"the substance of things hoped for, the
evidence of things not seen." Under her delicately etched
brows they glowed like two stars, their dancing lights half
hidden in lustrous darkness. They had never been ac-
counted for, Rebecca's eyes. The school-teacher and the
minister at Temperance had tried and failed; the young
artist who came for the summer to sketch the red barn, the
ruined mill, and the bridge ended by giving up all these
local beauties and devoting herself to the face of a child—
a small, plain face illuminated by a pair of eyes carrying
such messages, such suggestions, such hints of sleeping
power and insight, that one never tired of looking into their
shining depths.

Mr. Cobb made none of these generalizations; his remark
to his wife that night was simply to the effect that whenever
the child looked at him she knocked him galley-west.

"Miss Ross, a lady that paints, gave me the sunshade,"
said Rebecca, when she had exchanged looks with Mr. Cobb

and learned his face by heart. "Did you notice the pinked double ruffle and the white tip and handle? They're ivory. The handle is scarred, you see. That's because Fanny sucked and chewed it in meeting when I wasn't looking. I've never felt the same to Fanny since."

"Is Fanny your sister?"

"She's one of them."

"How many are there of you?"

"Seven. There's verses written about seven children:—

> "Quick was the little Maid's reply,
>   O master! we are seven!

I learned it to speak in school, but the scholars were hateful and laughed. Hannah is the oldest, I come next, then John, then Jenny, then Mark, then Fanny, then Mira."

"Well, that *is* a big family!"

"Far too big, everybody says," replied Rebecca with an unexpected and thoroughly grown-up candor that induced Mr. Cobb to murmur, "I swan!" and insert more tobacco in his left cheek.

"They're dear, but such a bother, and cost so much to feed, you see," she rippled on. "Hannah and I haven't done anything but put babies to bed at night and take them up in the morning for years and years. But it's finished, that's one comfort, and we'll have a lovely time when we're all grown up and the mortgage is paid off."

"All finished? Oh, you mean you've come away?"

"No, I mean they're all over and done with; our family's finished. Mother says so, and she always keeps her promises. There hasn't been any since Mira, and she's three. She was

born the day father died. Aunt Miranda wanted Hannah to
come to Riverboro instead of me, but mother couldn't spare
her; she takes hold of housework better than I do, Hannah
does. I told mother last night if there was likely to be any
more children while I was away I'd have to be sent for, for
when there's a baby it always takes Hannah and me both,
for mother has the cooking and the farm."

"Oh, you live on a farm, do ye? Where is it?—near to
where you got on?"

"Near? Why, it must be thousands of miles! We came
from Temperance in the cars. Then we drove a long ways
to Cousin Ann's and went to bed. Then we got up and drove
ever so far to Maplewood, where the stage was. Our farm
is away off from everywheres, but our school and meeting-
house is at Temperance, and that's only two miles. Sitting
up here with you is 'most as good as climbing the meeting-
house steeple. I know a boy who's been up on our steeple.
He said the people and cows looked like flies. We haven't
met any people yet, but I'm *kind* of disappointed in the
cows—they don't look so little as I hoped they would; still"
(brightening) "they don't look quite as big as if we were
down side of them, do they? Boys always do the nice splendid things, and girls can only do the nasty dull ones that get
left over. They can't climb so high, or go so far, or stay out
so late, or run so fast, or anything."

Mr. Cobb wiped his mouth on the back of his hand and
gasped. He had a feeling that he was being hurried from
peak to peak of a mountain range without time to take a
good breath in between.

"I can't seem to locate your farm," he said, "though I've

been to Temperance and used to live up that way. What's your folks' name?"

"Randall. My mother's name is Aurelia Randall; our names are Hannah Lucy Randall, Rebecca Rowena Randall, John Halifax Randall, Jenny Lind Randall, Marquis Randall, Fanny Ellsler Randall, and Miranda Randall. Mother named half of us and father the other half, but we didn't come out even, so they both thought it would be nice to name Mira after Aunt Miranda in Riverboro; they hoped it might do some good, but it didn't, and now we call her Mira. We are all named after somebody in particular. Hannah is 'Hannah at the Window Binding Shoes,' and I am taken out of 'Ivanhoe'; John Halifax was a gentleman in a book; Mark is after his uncle, Marquis de Lafayette, that died a twin. (Twins very often don't live to grow up, and triplets almost never—did you know that, Mr. Cobb?) We don't call him Marquis, only Mark. Jenny is named for a singer and Fanny for a beautiful dancer, but mother says they're both misfits, for Jenny can't carry a tune and Fanny's kind of stiff-legged. Mother would like to call them Jane and Frances and give up their middle names, but she says it wouldn't be fair to father. She says we must always stand up for father, because everything was against him, and he wouldn't have died if he hadn't had such bad luck. I think that's all there is to tell about us," she finished seriously.

"Land o' Liberty! I should think it was enough," ejaculated Mr. Cobb. "There wa'n't many names left when your mother got through choosin'! You've got a powerful good memory! I guess it ain't no trouble for you to learn your lessons, is it?"

"Not much; the trouble is to get the shoes to go and learn 'em. These are spandy new I've got on, and they have to last six months. Mother always says to save my shoes. There don't seem to be any way of saving shoes but taking 'em off and going barefoot; but I can't do that in Riverboro without shaming Aunt Mirandy. I'm going to school right along now when I'm living with Aunt Mirandy, and in two years I'm going to the seminary at Wareham; mother says it ought to be the making of me! I'm going to be a painter like Miss Ross when I get through school. At any rate, that's what *I* think I'm going to be. Mother thinks I'd better teach."

"Your farm ain't the old Hobbs place, is it?"

"No, it's just Randall's Farm. At least that's what mother calls it. I call it Sunnybrook Farm."

"I guess it don't make no difference what you call it so long as you know where it is," remarked Mr. Cobb sententiously.

Rebecca turned the full light of her eyes upon him reproachfully, almost severely, as she answered:—

"Oh! don't say that, and be like all the rest! It does make a difference what you call things. When I say Randall's Farm, do you see how it looks?"

"No, I can't say I do," responded Mr. Cobb uneasily.

"Now when I say Sunnybrook Farm, what does it make you think of?"

Mr. Cobb felt like a fish removed from his native element and left panting on the sand; there was no evading the awful responsibility of a reply, for Rebecca's eyes were searchlights that pierced the fiction of his brain and perceived the bald spot on the back of his head.

"I s'pose there's a brook somewheres near it," he said timorously.

Rebecca looked disappointed but not quite disheartened. "That's pretty good," she said encouragingly. "You're warm but not hot; there's a brook, but not a common brook. It has young trees and baby bushes on each side of it, and it's a shallow chattering little brook with a white sandy bottom and lots of little shiny pebbles. Whenever there's a bit of sunshine the brook catches it, and it's always full of sparkles the livelong day. Don't your stomach feel hollow? Mine does! I was so 'fraid I'd miss the stage I couldn't eat any breakfast."

"You'd better have your lunch, then. I don't eat nothin' till I get to Milltown; then I get a piece o' pie and cup o' coffee."

"I wish I could see Milltown. I suppose it's bigger and grander even than Wareham; more like Paris? Miss Ross told me about Paris; she bought my pink sunshade there and my bead purse. You see how it opens with a snap? I've twenty cents in it, and it's got to last three months, for stamps and paper and ink. Mother says Aunt Mirandy won't want to buy things like those when she's feeding and clothing me and paying for my school-books."

"Paris ain't no great," said Mr. Cobb disparagingly. "It's the dullest place in the State o' Maine. I've druv there many a time."

Again Rebecca was obliged to reprove Mr. Cobb, tacitly and quietly, but none the less surely, though the reproof was dealt with one glance, quickly sent and as quickly withdrawn.

"Paris is the capital of France, and you have to go to it on a boat," she said instructively. "It's in my geography, and it says: 'The French are a gay and polite people, fond of dancing and light wines.' I asked the teacher what light wines were, and he thought it was something like new cider, or maybe ginger pop. I can see Paris as plain as day by just shutting my eyes. But you can see Milltown 'most every day with your eyes wide open," Rebecca said wistfully.

"Milltown ain't no great, neither," replied Mr. Cobb, with the air of having visited all the cities of the earth and found them as naught. "Now you watch me heave this newspaper right onto Mis' Brown's doorstep."

Piff! and the packet landed exactly as it was intended, on the corn-husk mat in front of the screen door.

"Oh, how splendid that was!" cried Rebecca with enthusiasm.

"I might fail on some of 'em, you know," said Mr. Cobb, beaming with modest pride. "If your Aunt Mirandy'll let you, I'll take you down to Milltown some day this summer when the stage ain't full."

A thrill of delicious excitement ran through Rebecca's frame, from her new shoes up, up to the leghorn cap and down the black braid. She pressed Mr. Cobb's knee ardently and said in a voice choking with tears of joy and astonishment, "Oh, it can't be true, it can't; to think I should see Milltown. It's like having a fairy godmother who asks you your wish and then gives it to you! Did you ever read 'Cinderella,' or 'The Yellow Dwarf,' or 'The Enchanted Frog,' or 'The Fair One with Golden Locks'?"

"No," said Mr. Cobb cautiously, after a moment's reflection. "I don't seem to think I ever did read jest those partic'lar ones. Where'd you get a chance at so much readin'?"

"Oh, I've read lots of books," answered Rebecca casually. "Father's and Miss Ross's and all the dif'rent school teachers', and all in the Sunday-School library. I've read 'The Lamplighter,' and 'Scottish Chiefs,' and 'Ivanhoe,' and 'The Heir of Redclyffe,' and 'Cora, the Doctor's Wife,' and 'David Copperfield,' and 'The Gold of Chickaree,' and 'Plutarch's Lives,' and 'Thaddeus of Warsaw,' and 'Pilgrim's Progress,' and lots more.—What have you read?"

"I've never happened to read those partic'lar books; but land! I've read a sight in my time! Nowadays I'm so drove I get along with the Almanac, the 'Weekly Argus,' and the 'Maine State Agriculturist.'—There's the river again; this is the last long hill, and when we get to the top of it we'll see the chimbleys of Riverboro in the distance. 'T ain't fur. I live 'bout half a mile beyond the brick house myself."

Rebecca's hand stirred nervously in her lap and she moved in her seat. "I didn't think I was going to be afraid," she said almost under her breath; "but I guess I am, just a little mite—when you say it's coming so near."

"Would you go back?" asked Mr. Cobb curiously.

She flashed him an intrepid look and then said proudly, "I'd never go back—I might be frightened, but I'd be ashamed to run. Going to Aunt Mirandy's is like going down cellar in the dark. There might be ogres and giants under the stairs,—but, as I tell Hannah, there *might* be elves and fairies and enchanted frogs!—Is there a main street in the village, like that in Wareham?"

"I s'pose you might call it a main street, an' your Aunt Sawyer lives on it, but there ain't no stores nor mills, an' it's an awful one-horse village!"

"I'm almost sorry," she sighed, "because it would be so grand to drive down a real main street, sitting high up like this behind two splendid horses, with my pink sunshade up, and everybody in town wondering who the bunch of lilacs and the hair trunk belongs to. It would be just like the beautiful lady in the parade. Last summer the circus came to Temperance, and they had a procession in the morning. And there were lovely horses and animals in cages, and clowns on horseback; and at the very end came a little red and gold chariot drawn by two ponies, and in it, sitting on a velvet cushion, was the snake charmer, all dressed in satin and spangles. She was so beautiful beyond compare, Mr. Cobb, that you had to swallow lumps in your throat when you looked at her, and little cold feelings crept up and down your back. Don't you know how I mean? Didn't you ever see anybody that made you feel like that?"

Mr. Cobb was more distinctly uncomfortable at this moment than he had been at any one time during the eventful morning, but he evaded the point dexterously by saying, "There ain't no harm, as I can see, in our makin' the grand entry in the biggest style we can. I'll take the whip out, set up straight, an' drive fast; you hold your bo'quet in your lap, an' open your little red parasol, an' we'll jest make the natives stare!"

The child's face was radiant for a moment, but the glow faded just as quickly as she said, "I forgot—Mother put me inside, and maybe she'd want me to be there when I got to

Aunt Mirandy's. Maybe I'd be more genteel inside, and then I wouldn't have to be jumped down and my clothes fly up, but could open the door and step down like a lady passenger. Would you please stop a minute, Mr. Cobb, and let me change?"

The stage-driver good-naturedly pulled up his horses, lifted the excited little creature down, opened the door, and helped her in, putting the lilacs and the pink sunshade beside her.

"We've had a great trip," he said, "and we've got real well acquainted, haven't we?—You won't forget about Milltown?"

"Never!" she exclaimed fervently; "and you're sure you won't either?"

"Never! Cross my heart!" vowed Mr. Cobb solemnly, as he remounted his perch.

And as the stage rumbled down the village street between the green maples, those who looked from their windows saw a little brown elf in buff calico sitting primly on the back seat holding a great bouquet tightly in one hand and a pink parasol in the other. Had they been far-sighted enough they might have seen, when the stage turned into the side dooryard of the old brick house, a calico yoke rising and falling tempestuously over the beating heart beneath, the red color coming and going in two pale cheeks, and a mist of tears swimming in two brilliant dark eyes.

Rebecca's journey had ended.

"There's the stage turnin' into the Sawyer girls' dooryard," said Mrs. Perkins to her husband. "That must be the niece from up Temperance way. It seems they wrote to Aurelia and invited Hannah, the oldest, but Aurelia said she could spare Rebecca better, if 't was all the same to Mirandy an' Jane; so it's Rebecca that's come. She'll be good comp'ny for our Emma Jane, but I don't believe they'll keep her three months! She looks black as an Injun what I can see of her; black and kind of up-an'-comin'. They used to say that one o' the Randalls married a Spanish woman, somebody that was teachin' music and languages at a boardin' school. Lorenzo was dark complected, you remember, and this child is, too. Well, I don't know as Spanish blood is any real disgrace, not if it's a good ways back and the woman was respectable."

Chapter Two

Rebecca's Relations

They had been called the Sawyer girls when Miranda at eighteen, Jane at twelve, and Aurelia at eight participated in the various activities of village life; and when Riverboro fell into a habit of thought or speech, it saw no reason for falling out of it; at any rate, in the same century. So although Miranda and Jane were between fifty and sixty at the time this story opens, Riverboro still called them the Sawyer girls. They were spinsters; but Aurelia, the youngest, had made what she called a romantic marriage and what her sisters termed a mighty poor speculation. "There's worse things than bein' old maids," they said; whether they thought so is quite another matter.

The element of romance in Aurelia's marriage existed chiefly in the fact that Mr. L. D. M. Randall had a soul above farming or trading and was a votary of the Muses. He taught the weekly singing-school (then a feature of village life) in half a dozen neighboring towns, he played the violin and "called off" at dances, or evoked rich harmonies from church melodeons on Sundays. He taught certain uncouth lads, when they were of an age to enter society, the intricacies of contra dances, or the steps of the schottische and mazurka, and he was a marked figure in all social assemblies, though conspicuously absent from town-meetings and the purely masculine gatherings at the store or tavern or bridge.

His hair was a little longer, his hands a little whiter, his shoes a little thinner, his manner a trifle more polished, than that of his soberer mates; indeed the only department of life in which he failed to shine was the making of sufficient money to live upon. Luckily he had no responsibilities; his father and his twin brother had died when he was yet a boy, and his mother, whose only noteworthy achievement had been the naming of her twin sons Marquis de Lafayette and Lorenzo de Medici Randall, had supported herself and educated her child by making coats up to the very day of her death. She was wont to say plaintively, "I'm afraid the faculties was too much divided up between my twins. L. D. M. is awful talented, but I guess M. D. L. would 'a' been the practical one if he'd 'a' lived."

"L. D. M. was practical enough to get the richest girl in the village," replied Mrs. Robinson.

"Yes," sighed his mother, "there it is again; if the twins could 'a' married Aurelia Sawyer, 't would 'a' been all right. L. D. M. was talented 'nough to *get* Reely's money, but M. D. L. would 'a' ben practical 'nough to have *kep'* it."

Aurelia's share of the modest Sawyer property had been put into one thing after another by the handsome and luckless Lorenzo de Medici. He had a graceful and poetic way of making an investment for each new son and daughter that blessed their union. "A birthday present for our child, Aurelia," he would say,—"a little nest-egg for the future." But Aurelia once remarked in a moment of bitterness that the hen never lived that could sit on those eggs and hatch anything out of them.

Miranda and Jane had virtually washed their hands of Aurelia when she married Lorenzo de Medici Randall. Having exhausted the resources of Riverboro and its immediate vicinity, the unfortunate couple had moved on and on in a steadily decreasing scale of prosperity until they had reached Temperance, where they had settled down and invited fate to do its worst, an invitation which was promptly accepted. The maiden sisters at home wrote to Aurelia two or three times a year, and sent modest but serviceable presents to the children at Christmas, but refused to assist L. D. M. with the regular expenses of his rapidly growing family. His last investment, made shortly before the birth of Miranda (named in a lively hope of favors which never came), was a small farm two miles from Temperance. Aurelia managed this herself, and so it proved a home at least, and a place for the unsuccessful Lorenzo to die and to be buried from, a duty somewhat too long deferred, many thought, which he performed on the day of Mira's birth.

It was in this happy-go-lucky household that Rebecca had grown up. It was just an ordinary family; two or three of the children were handsome and the rest plain, three of them rather clever, two industrious, and two commonplace and dull. Rebecca had her father's facility and had been his aptest pupil. She "carried" the alto by ear, danced without being taught, played the melodeon without knowing the notes. Her love of books she inherited chiefly from her mother, who found it hard to sweep or cook or sew when there was a novel in the house. Fortunately books were scarce, or the children might sometimes have gone ragged and hungry.

But other forces had been at work in Rebecca, and the traits of unknown forbears had been wrought into her fiber. Lorenzo de Medici was flabby and boneless; Rebecca was a thing of fire and spirit: he lacked energy and courage; Rebecca was plucky at two and dauntless at five. Mrs. Randall and Hannah had no sense of humor; Rebecca possessed and showed it as soon as she could walk and talk.

She had not been able, however, to borrow her parents' virtues and those of other generous ancestors and escape all the weaknesses in the calendar. She had not her sister Hannah's patience or her brother John's sturdy staying power. Her will was sometimes willfulness, and the ease with which she did most things led her to be impatient of hard tasks or long ones. But whatever else there was or was not, there was freedom at Randall's farm. The children grew, worked, fought, ate what and slept where they could; loved one another and their parents pretty well, but with no tropical passion; and educated themselves for nine months of the year, each one in his own way.

As a result of this method Hannah, who could only have been developed by forces applied from without, was painstaking, humdrum, and limited; while Rebecca, who apparently needed nothing but space to develop in, and a knowledge of terms in which to express herself, grew and grew and grew, always from within outward. Her forces of one sort and another had seemingly been set in motion when she was born; they needed no daily spur, but moved of their own accord—towards what no one knew, least of all Rebecca herself. The field for the exhibition of her creative instinct was painfully small, and the only use she had made of it as yet was to leave eggs out of the corn bread one day and milk another, to see how it would turn out; to part Fanny's hair sometimes in the middle, sometimes on the right, and sometimes on the left side; and to play all sorts of fantastic pranks with the children, occasionally bringing them to the table as fictitious or historical characters found in her favorite books. Rebecca amused her mother and her family generally, but she never was counted of serious importance, and though considered "smart" and old for her age, she was never thought superior in any way. Aurelia's experience of genius, as exemplified in the deceased Lorenzo de Medici, led her into a greater admiration of plain, everyday common sense, a quality in which Rebecca, it must be confessed, seemed sometimes painfully deficient.

Hannah was her mother's favorite, so far as Aurelia could indulge herself in such recreations as partiality. The parent who is obliged to feed and clothe seven children on an income of fifteen dollars a month seldom has time to discriminate carefully between the various members of her brood, but Hannah at fourteen was at once companion and partner in all her mother's problems. She it was who kept the house while Aurelia busied herself in barn and field. Rebecca was capable of certain set tasks, such as keeping the small children from killing themselves and one another, feeding the poultry, picking up chips, hulling strawberries, wiping

dishes; but she was thought irresponsible, and Aurelia, need-
ing somebody to lean on (having never enjoyed that luxury
with the gifted Lorenzo), leaned on Hannah. Hannah
showed the result of this attitude somewhat, being a trifle
careworn in face and sharp in manner; but she was a self-
contained, well-behaved, dependable child, and that is the
reason her aunts had invited her to Riverboro to be a member of their family and participate in all the advantages of
their loftier position in the world. It was several years since
Miranda and Jane had seen the children, but they remembered with pleasure that Hannah had not spoken a word
during the interview, and it was for this reason that they
had asked for the pleasure of her company. Rebecca, on the
other hand, had dressed up the dog in John's clothes, and
being requested to get the three younger children ready for
dinner, she had held them under the pump and then proceeded to "smack" their hair flat to their heads by vigorous
brushing, bringing them to the table in such a moist and
hideous state of shininess that their mother was ashamed
of their appearance. Rebecca's own black locks were commonly pushed smoothly off her forehead, but on this occasion she formed what I must perforce call by its only name, a
"spit-curl," directly in the center of her brow, an ornament
which she was allowed to wear a very short time, only in fact
till Hannah was able to call her mother's attention to it,
when she was sent into the next room to remove it and come
back looking like a Christian. This command she interpreted
somewhat too literally, perhaps, because she contrived in
a space of two minutes an extremely pious style of hairdress-
ing, fully as effective if not as startling as the first. These

antics were solely the result of nervous irritation, a mood
born of Miss Miranda Sawyer's stiff, grim, and martial attitude.

The remembrance of Rebecca was so vivid that their sister
Aurelia's letter was something of a shock to the quiet, elderly
spinsters of the brick house; for it said that Hannah could
not possibly be spared for a few years yet, but that Rebecca
would come as soon as she could be made ready; that the
offer was most thankfully appreciated, and that the regular
schooling and church privileges, as well as the influence of
the Sawyer home, would doubtless be "the making of Rebecca."

Chapter Three

A Difference in Hearts

I don' know as I cal'lated to be the makin' of any child," Miranda had said as she folded Aurelia's letter and laid it in the lightstand drawer. "I s'posed, of course, Aurelia would send us the one we asked for, but it's just like her to palm off that wild young one on somebody else."

"You remember we said that Rebecca or even Jenny might come, in case Hannah couldn't," interposed Jane.

"I know we did, but we hadn't any notion it would turn out that way," grumbled Miranda.

"She was a mite of a thing when we saw her three years ago," ventured Jane; "she's had time to improve."

"And time to grow worse!"

"Won't it be kind of a privilege to put her on the right track?" asked Jane timidly.

"I don' know about the privilege part; it'll be considerable of a chore, I guess. If her mother hain't got her on the right track by now, she won't take to it herself all of a sudden."

This depressed and depressing frame of mind had lasted

until the eventful day dawned on which Rebecca was to arrive.

"If she makes as much work after she comes as she has before, we might as well give up hope of ever gettin' any rest," sighed Miranda as she hung the dish towels on the barberry bushes at the side door.

"But we should have had to clean house, Rebecca or no Rebecca," urged Jane; "and I can't see why you've scrubbed and washed and baked as you have for that one child, nor why you've about bought out Watson's stock of dry goods."

"I know Aurelia if you don't," responded Miranda. "I've seen her house, and I've seen that batch o' children, wearin' one another's clothes and never carin' whether they had 'em on right sid' out or not; I know what they've had to live and dress on, and so do you. That child will like as not come with a passel o' things borrowed from the rest o' the family. She'll have Hannah's shoes and John's undershirts and Mark's socks most likely. I suppose she never had a thimble on her finger in her life, but she'll know the feelin' o' one before she's ben here many days. I've bought a piece of unbleached muslin and a piece o' brown gingham for her to make up; that'll keep her busy. Of course she won't pick up anything after herself; she probably never saw a duster, and she'll be as hard to train into our ways as if she was a heathen."

"She'll make a dif'rence," acknowledged Jane, "but she may turn out more biddable 'n we think."

"She'll mind when she's spoken to, biddable or not," remarked Miranda with a shake of the last towel.

Miranda Sawyer had a heart, of course, but she had never used it for any other purpose than the pumping and circulating of blood. She was just, conscientious, economical, industrious; a regular attendant at church and Sunday-School, and a member of the State Missionary and Bible Societies, but in the presence of all these chilly virtues you longed for one warm little fault, or lacking that, one likable failing, something to make you sure she was thoroughly alive. She had never had any education other than that of the neighborhood district school, for her desires and ambitions had all pointed to the management of the house, the farm, and the dairy. Jane, on the other hand, had gone to an academy, and also to a boarding-school for young ladies; so had Aurelia; and after all the years that had elapsed there was still a slight difference in language and in manner between the elder and the two younger sisters.

Jane, too, had had the inestimable advantage of a sorrow; not the natural grief at the loss of her aged father and mother, for she had been content to let them go; but something far deeper. She was engaged to marry young Tom Carter, who had nothing to marry on, it is true, but who was sure to have, some time or other. Then the war broke out. Tom enlisted at the first call. Up to that time Jane had loved him with a quiet, friendly sort of affection, and had given her country a mild emotion of the same sort. But the strife, the danger, the anxiety of the time, set new currents of feeling in motion. Life became something other than the three meals a day, the round of cooking, washing, sewing, and church-going. Personal gossip vanished from the village conversation. Big things took the place of trifling ones,—

sacred sorrows of wives and mothers, pangs of fathers and husbands' self-denials, sympathies, new desires to bear one another's burdens. Men and women grew fast in those days of the nation's trouble and danger, and Jane awoke from the vague dull dream she had hitherto called life to new hopes, new fears, new purposes. Then after a year's anxiety, a year when one never looked in the newspaper without dread and sickness of suspense, came the telegram saying that Tom was wounded; and without so much as asking Miranda's leave, she packed her trunk and started for the South. She was in time to hold Tom's hand through hours of pain; to show him for once the heart of a prim New England girl when it is ablaze with love and grief; to put her arms about him so that he could have a home to die in, and that was all; —all, but it served.

It carried her through weary months of nursing—nursing of other soldiers for Tom's dear sake; it sent her home a better woman; and though she had never left Riverboro in all the years that lay between, and had grown into the counterfeit presentment of her sister and of all other thin, spare, New England spinsters, it was something of a counterfeit, and underneath was still the faint echo of that wild heartbeat of her girlhood. Having learned the trick of beating and loving and suffering, the poor faithful heart persisted, although it lived on memories and carried on its sentimental operations mostly in secret.

"You're soft, Jane," said Miranda once; "you allers was soft, and you allers will be. If 't wa'n't for me keeping you stiffened up, I b'lieve you'd leak out o' the house into the dooryard."

It was already past the appointed hour for Mr. Cobb and his coach to be lumbering down the street.

"The stage ought to be here," said Miranda, glancing nervously at the tall clock for the twentieth time. "I guess everything's done. I've tacked up two thick towels back of her washstand and put a mat under her slop-jar; but children are awful hard on furniture. I expect we sha'n't know this house a year from now."

Jane's frame of mind was naturally depressed and timorous, having been affected by Miranda's gloomy presages of evil to come. The only difference between the sisters in this matter was that while Miranda only wondered how they could endure Rebecca, Jane had flashes of inspiration in which she wondered how Rebecca would endure them. It was in one of these flashes that she ran up the back stairs to put a vase of apple blossoms and a red tomato-pincushion on Rebecca's bureau.

The stage rumbled to the side door of the brick house, and Mr. Cobb handed Rebecca out like a real lady passenger. She alighted with great circumspection, put the bunch of faded flowers in her Aunt Miranda's hand, and received her salute; it could hardly be called a kiss without injuring the fair name of that commodity.

"You needn't 'a' bothered to bring flowers," remarked that gracious and tactful lady; "the garden's always full of 'em here when it comes time."

Jane then kissed Rebecca, giving a somewhat better imitation of the real thing than her sister. "Put the trunk in the entry, Jeremiah, and we'll get it carried upstairs this afternoon," she said.

"I'll take it up for ye now, if ye say the word, girls."

"No, no; don't leave the horses; somebody'll be comin' past, and we can call 'em in."

"Well, good-bye, Rebecca; good-day, Mirandy 'n' Jane. You've got a lively little girl there. I guess she'll be a first-rate company keeper."

Miss Sawyer shuddered openly at the adjective "lively" as applied to a child; her belief being that though children might be seen, if absolutely necessary, they certainly should never be heard if she could help it. "We're not much used to noise, Jane and me," she remarked acidly.

Mr. Cobb saw that he had taken the wrong tack, but he was too unused to argument to explain himself readily, so he drove away, trying to think by what safer word than "lively" he might have described his interesting little passenger.

"I'll take you up and show you your room, Rebecca," Miss Miranda said. "Shut the mosquito-nettin' door tight behind you, so's to keep the flies out; it ain't flytime yet, but I want you to start right; take your passel along with ye and then you won't have to come down for it; always make your head save your heels. Rub your feet on that braided rug; hang your hat and cape in the entry there as you go past."

"It's my best hat," said Rebecca.

"Take it upstairs then and put it in the clothes-press; but I shouldn't 'a' thought you'd 'a' worn your best hat on the stage."

"It's my only hat," explained Rebecca. "My every-day hat wasn't good enough to bring. Fanny's going to finish it."

"Lay your parasol in the entry closet."

"Do you mind if I keep it in my room, please? It always seems safer."

"There ain't any thieves hereabouts, and if there was, I guess they wouldn't make for your sunshade; but come along. Remember to always go up the back way; we don't use the front stairs on account o' the carpet; take care o' the turn and don't ketch your foot; look to your right and go in. When you've washed your face and hands and brushed your hair you can come down, and by and by we'll unpack your trunk and get you settled before supper. Ain't you got your dress on hind sid' foremost?"

Rebecca drew her chin down and looked at the row of smoked pearl buttons running up and down the middle of her flat little chest.

"Hind side foremost? Oh, I see! No, that's all right. If you have seven children you can't keep buttonin' and un-buttonin' 'em all the time—they have to do themselves. We're always buttoned up in front at our house. Mira's only three, but she's buttoned up in front, too."

Miranda said nothing as she closed the door, but her looks were at once equivalent to and more eloquent than words.

Rebecca stood perfectly still in the center of the floor and looked about her. There was a square of oilcloth in front of each article of furniture and a drawn-in rug beside the single four poster, which was covered with a fringed white dimity counterpane.

Everything was as neat as wax, but the ceilings were much higher than Rebecca was accustomed to. It was a north room, and the window, which was long and narrow, looked out on the back buildings and the barn.

It was not the room, which was far more comfortable than Rebecca's own at the farm, nor the lack of view, nor yet the long journey, for she was not conscious of weariness; it was not the fear of a strange place, for she loved new places and courted new sensations; it was because of some curious blending of uncomprehended emotions that Rebecca stood her sunshade in the corner, tore off her best hat, flung it on the bureau with the porcupine quills on the underside, and stripping down the dimity spread, precipitated herself into the middle of the bed and pulled the counterpane over her head.

In a moment the door opened quietly. Knocking was a refinement quite unknown in Riverboro, and if it had been heard of would never have been wasted on a child.

Miss Miranda entered, and as her eye wandered about the vacant room, it fell upon a white and tempestuous ocean of counterpane, an ocean breaking into strange movements of wave and crest and billow.

"*Rebecca!*"

The tone in which the word was voiced gave it all the effect of having been shouted from the housetops.

A dark ruffled head and two frightened eyes appeared above the dimity spread.

"What are you layin' on your good bed in the daytime for, messin' up the feathers, and dirtyin' the pillers with your dusty boots?"

Rebecca rose guiltily. There seemed no excuse to make. Her offense was beyond explanation or apology.

"I'm sorry, Aunt Mirandy—something came over me; I don't know what."

"Well, if it comes over you very soon again we'll have to

find out what 't is. Spread your bed up smooth this minute,
for 'Bijah Flagg's bringin' your trunk upstairs, and I wouldn't
let him see such a cluttered-up room for anything; he'd tell
it all over town."

When Mr. Cobb had put up his horses that night he carried a kitchen chair to the side of his wife, who was sitting
on the back porch.

"I brought a little Randall girl down on the stage from
Maplewood to-day, Mother. She's kin to the Sawyer girls
an' is goin' to live with 'em," he said, as he sat down and began to whittle. "She's that Aurelia's child, the one that ran
away with Susan Randall's son just before we come here to
live."

"How old a child?"

" 'Bout ten, or somewhere along there, an' small for her
age; but land! she might be a hundred to hear her talk! She
kep' me jumpin' tryin' to answer her! Of all the queer children I ever come across she's the queerest. She ain't no
beauty—her face is all eyes; but if she ever grows up to them
eyes an' fills out a little she'll make folks stare. Land,
Mother! I wish 't you could 'a' heard her talk."

"I don't see what she had to talk about, a child like that,
to a stranger," replied Mrs. Cobb.

"Stranger or no stranger, 't wouldn't make no difference
to her. She'd talk to a pump or a grindstun; she'd talk to
herself ruther'n keep still."

"What did she talk about?"

"Blamed if I can repeat any of it. She kep' me so surprised
I didn't have my wits about me. She had a little pink sun-

shade—it kind o' looked like a doll's amberill, 'n' she clung to it like a burr to a woolen stockin'. I advised her to open it up—the sun was so hot; but she said no, 't would fade, an' she tucked it under her dress. 'It's the dearest thing in life to me,' says she, 'but it's a dreadful care.' Them's the very words, an' it's all the words I remember. 'It's the dearest thing in life to me, but it's an awful care!'" Here Mr. Cobb laughed aloud as he tipped his chair back against the side of the house. "There was another thing, but I can't get it right exactly. She was talkin' 'bout the circus parade an' the snake charmer in a gold chariot, an' says she, 'She was so beautiful beyond compare, Mr. Cobb, that it made you have lumps in your throat to look at her.' She'll be comin' over to see you, Mother, an' you can size her up for yourself. I don' know how she'll git on with Mirandy Sawyer— poor little soul!"

This doubt was more or less openly expressed in Riverboro, which, however, had two opinions on the subject; one that it was a most generous thing in the Sawyer girls to take one of Aurelia's children to educate, the other that the education would be bought at a price wholly out of proportion to its intrinsic value.

Chapter Four

Wisdom's Ways

The day of Rebecca's arrival had been Friday, and on the Monday following she began her education at the school which was in Riverboro Center, about a mile distant. Miss Sawyer borrowed a neighbor's horse and wagon and drove to the schoolhouse, interviewing the teacher, Miss Dearborn, arranging for books, and generally starting the child on a path that was to lead to boundless knowledge.

Rebecca walked to school after the first morning. She loved this part of the day's programme. When the dew was not too heavy and the weather was fair there was a short cut through the woods. She turned off the main road, crept through Uncle Josh Woodman's bars, waved away Mrs. Carter's cows, trod the short grass of the pasture, with its well-worn path running through gardens of buttercups and whiteweed, and groves of ivory leaves and sweet fern. She descended a little hill, jumped from stone to stone across a woodland brook, startling the drowsy frogs, who were always winking and blinking in the morning sun. Then came the "woodsy bit," with her feet pressing the slippery carpet of brown pine needles; the "woodsy bit" so full of dewy morning surprises.—Then she climbed a stile, went through a grassy meadow, slid under another pair of bars, and came out into the road again, having gained nearly half a mile.

How delicious it all was! Rebecca clasped her Quackenbos's Grammar and Greenleaf's Arithmetic with a joyful sense of knowing her lessons. Her dinner pail swung from her right hand, and she had a blissful consciousness of the two soda biscuits spread with butter and syrup, the baked cup-custard, the doughnut, and the square of hard gingerbread. Sometimes she said whatever "piece" she was going to speak on the next Friday afternoon.

A soldier of the Legion lay dying in Algiers,
There was lack of woman's nursing, there was dearth of woman's
    tears.

How she loved the swing and the sentiment of it! How her young voice quivered whenever she came to the refrain:—

But we'll meet no more at Bingen, dear Bingen on the Rhine.

It always sounded beautiful in her ears, as she sent her tearful little treble into the clear morning air. Another early favorite (for we must remember that Rebecca's only knowledge of the great world of poetry consisted of the selections in vogue in school readers) was:—

> Woodman, spare that tree!
>   Touch not a single bough!
>   In youth it sheltered me,
>   And I'll protect it now.

When Emma Jane Perkins walked through the "short cut" with her, the two children used to render this with appropriate dramatic action. Emma Jane always chose to be the woodman because she had nothing to do but raise on high an imaginary axe.

At the last pair of bars the two girls were sometimes met by a detachment of the Simpson children, who lived in a black house with a red door and a red barn behind, on the Blueberry Plains road. Rebecca felt an interest in the Simpsons from the first, because there were so many of them and they were so patched and darned, just like her own brood at the home farm.

The little schoolhouse with its flagpole on top and its two doors in front, one for boys and the other for girls, stood on the crest of a hill, with rolling fields and meadows on one side, a stretch of pine woods on the other, and the river glinting and sparkling in the distance. It boasted no attractions within. All was as bare and ugly and uncomfortable as it well could be, for the villages along the river expended so much money in repairing and rebuilding bridges that they were obliged to be very economical in school privileges. The teacher's desk and chair stood on a platform in one corner; there was an uncouth stove, never blackened oftener than once a year, a map of the United States, two blackboards, a ten-quart tin pail of water and long-handled dipper on a corner shelf, and wooden desks and benches for the scholars, who only numbered twenty in Rebecca's time. The seats were higher in the back of the room, and the more advanced and longer-legged pupils sat there, the position being greatly to be envied, as they were at once nearer to the windows and farther from the teacher.

There were classes of a sort, although nobody, broadly

speaking, studied the same book with anybody else, or had arrived at the same degree of proficiency in any one branch of learning. Rebecca in particular was so difficult to classify that Miss Dearborn at the end of a fortnight gave up the attempt altogether. She read with Dick Carter and Living Perkins, who were fitting for the academy; recited arithmetic with lisping little Thuthan Thimpthon; geography with Emma Jane Perkins, and grammar after school hours to Miss Dearborn alone. Full to the brim as she was of clever thoughts and quaint fancies, she made at first but a poor hand at composition. The labor of writing and spelling, with the added difficulties of punctuation and capitals, interfered sadly with the free expression of ideas. She took history with Alice Robinson's class, which was attacking the subject of the Revolution, while Rebecca was bidden to begin with the discovery of America. In a week she had mastered the course of events up to the Revolution, and in ten days had arrived at Yorktown, where the class had apparently established summer quarters. Then finding that extra effort would only result in her reciting with the oldest Simpson boy, she deliberately held herself back, for wisdom's ways were not those of pleasantness nor her paths those of peace if one were compelled to tread them in the company of "Seesaw" Simpson. Samuel Simpson was generally called "Seesaw," because of his difficulty in making up his mind. Whether it were a question of fact, of spelling, or of date, of going swimming or fishing, of choosing a book in the Sunday-School library or a stick of candy at the village store, he had no sooner determined on one plan of action than his wish fondly reverted to the opposite one. Seesaw was pale, flaxen-haired, blue-eyed, round-shouldered, and given to stammering when nervous. Perhaps because of his very weakness Rebecca's decision of character had a fascination for him, and although she snubbed him to the verge of madness, he could never keep his eyes away from her. The force with which she tied her shoe when the lacing came undone, the flirt over shoulder she gave her black braid when she was excited or warm, her manner of studying,—book on desk, arms folded, eyes fixed on the opposite wall,—all had an abiding charm for Seesaw Simpson. When, having obtained permission, she walked to the water pail in the corner and drank from the dipper, unseen forces dragged Seesaw from his seat to go and drink after her. It was not only that there was something akin to association and intimacy in drinking next, but there was the fearful joy of meeting her in transit and receiving a cold and disdainful look from her wonderful eyes.

On a certain warm day in summer Rebecca's thirst exceeded the bounds of propriety. When she asked a third time for permission to quench it at the common fountain Miss Dearborn nodded "yes," but lifted her eyebrows unpleasantly as Rebecca neared the desk. As she replaced the dipper Seesaw promptly raised his hand, and Miss Dearborn indicated a weary affirmative.

"What is the matter with you, Rebecca?" she asked.

"I had salt mackerel for breakfast," answered Rebecca.

There seemed nothing humorous about this reply, which was merely the statement of a fact, but an irrepressible titter ran through the school. Miss Dearborn did not enjoy jokes neither made nor understood by herself, and her face flushed.

"I think you had better stand by the pail for five minutes, Rebecca; it may help you to control your thirst."

Rebecca's heart fluttered. She to stand in the corner by the water pail and be stared at by all the scholars! She unconsciously made a gesture of angry dissent and moved a step nearer her seat, but was arrested by Miss Dearborn's command in a still firmer voice.

"Stand by the pail, Rebecca! Samuel, how many times have you asked for water to-day?"

"This is the f-f-fourth."

"Don't touch the dipper, please. The school has done nothing but drink this afternoon; it has had no time whatever to study. I suppose you had something salt for breakfast, Samuel?" queried Miss Dearborn with sarcasm.

"I had m-m-mackerel, j-just like Reb-b-becca." (Irrepressible giggles by the school.)

"I judged so. Stand by the other side of the pail, Samuel."

Rebecca's head was bowed with shame and wrath. Life looked too black a thing to be endured. The punishment was bad enough, but to be coupled in correction with Seesaw Simpson was beyond human endurance.

Singing was the last exercise in the afternoon, and Minnie Smellie chose "Shall We Gather at the River?" It was a baleful choice and seemed to hold some secret and subtle association with the situation and general progress of events; or at any rate there was apparently some obscure reason for the energy and vim with which the scholars shouted the choral invitation again and again:—

Shall we gather at the river,
The beautiful, the beautiful river?

Miss Dearborn stole a look at Rebecca's bent head and
was frightened. The child's face was pale save for two red
spots glowing on her cheeks. Tears hung on her lashes; her
breath came and went quickly, and the hand that held her
pocket handkerchief trembled like a leaf.

"You may go to your seat, Rebecca," said Miss Dearborn
at the end of the first song. "Samuel, stay where you are till
the close of school. And let me tell you, scholars, that I asked
Rebecca to stand by the pail only to break up this habit of
incessant drinking, which is nothing but empty-mindedness
and desire to walk to and fro over the floor. Every time Rebecca has asked for a drink to-day the whole school has gone
to the pail one after another. She is really thirsty, and I dare
say I ought to have punished you for following her example,
not her for setting it. What shall we sing now, Alice?"

" 'The Old Oaken Bucket,' please."

"Think of something dry, Alice, and change the subject.
Yes, 'The Star-Spangled Banner' if you like, or anything
else."

Rebecca sank into her seat and pulled the singing-book
from her desk. Miss Dearborn's public explanation had
shifted some of the weight from her heart, and she felt a trifle
raised in her self-esteem.

Under cover of the general relaxation of singing, votive
offerings of respectful sympathy began to make their appearance at her shrine. Living Perkins, who could not sing,
dropped a piece of maple sugar in her lap as he passed her
on his way to the blackboard to draw the map of Maine.

Alice Robinson rolled a perfectly new slate pencil over the
floor with her foot until it reached Rebecca's place, while her
seat-mate, Emma Jane, had made up a little mound of paper
balls and labeled them "Bullets for you know who."

Altogether existence grew brighter, and when she was
left alone with the teacher for her grammar lesson she had
nearly recovered her equanimity, which was more than
Miss Dearborn had. The last clattering foot had echoed
through the hall, Seesaw's backward glance of penitence had
been met and answered defiantly by one of cold disdain.

"Rebecca, I am afraid I punished you more than I meant,"
said Miss Dearborn, who was only eighteen herself, and in
her year of teaching country schools had never encountered
a child like Rebecca.

"I hadn't missed a question this whole day, nor whispered either," quavered the culprit; "and I don't think I
ought to be ashamed just for drinking."

"You started all the others, or it seemed as if you did.
Whatever you do they all do, whether you laugh, or miss, or
write notes, or ask to leave the room, or drink; and it must be
stopped."

"Sam Simpson is a copy-cat!" stormed Rebecca. "I
wouldn't have minded standing in the corner alone—that is,
not so very much. But I couldn't bear standing with him."

"I saw that you couldn't, and that's the reason I told you
to take your seat, and left him in the corner. Remember that
you are a stranger in the place, and they take more notice of
what you do, so you must be careful. Now let's have our
conjugations. Give me the verb 'to be,' potential mood, past
perfect tense."

I might have been	We might have been
Thou mightst have been	You might have been
He might have been	They might have been.

"Give me an example, please."

I might have been glad
Thou mightst have been glad
He, she, or it might have been glad.

" 'He' or 'she' might have been glad because they are masculine and feminine, but could 'it' have been glad?" asked Miss Dearborn, who was very fond of splitting hairs.

"Why not?" asked Rebecca.

"Because 'it' is neuter gender."

"Couldn't we say, 'The kitten might have been glad if it had known it was not going to be drowned'?"

"Ye—es," Miss Dearborn answered hesitatingly, never very sure of herself under Rebecca's fire; "but though we often speak of a baby, a chicken, or a kitten as 'it,' they are really masculine or feminine gender, not neuter."

Rebecca reflected a long moment and then asked, "Is hollyhock neuter?"

"Oh, yes, of course it is, Rebecca."

"Well, couldn't we say, 'The hollyhock might have been glad to see the rain, but there was a weak little hollyhock bud growing out of its stalk and it was afraid that that might be hurt by the storm; so the big hollyhock was kind of afraid, instead of being real glad'?"

Miss Dearborn looked puzzled as she answered, "Of course, Rebecca, hollyhocks could not be sorry, or glad, or afraid, really."

"We can't tell, I s'pose," replied the child, "but *I* think they are, anyway. Now, what shall I say?"

"The subjunctive mood, past perfect tense of the verb 'to know.' "

If I had known	If we had known
If thou hadst known	If you had known
If he had known	If they had known.

"Oh, it is the saddest tense," sighed Rebecca with a little break in her voice; "nothing but *ifs, ifs, ifs!* It makes you feel that if they only *had* known, things might have been better!"

Miss Dearborn had not thought of it before, but on reflection she believed the subjunctive mood was a "sad" one and "if" rather a sorry "part of speech."

"Give me some more examples of the subjunctive, Rebecca, and that will do for this afternoon," she said.

"If I had not loved mackerel I should not have been thirsty," said Rebecca with an April smile, as she closed her grammar. "If thou hadst loved me truly thou wouldst not have stood me up in the corner. If Samuel had not loved wickedness he would not have followed me to the water pail."

"And if Rebecca had loved the rules of the school she would have controlled her thirst," finished Miss Dearborn with a kiss, and the two parted friends.

Chapter Five

Sunshine in a Shady Place

The little schoolhouse on the hill had its moments of triumph as well as its scenes of tribulation, but it was fortunate that Rebecca had her books and her new acquaintances to keep her interested and occupied, or life would have gone heavily with her that first summer in Riverboro. She tried to like her Aunt Miranda (the idea of loving her had been given up at the moment of meeting), but failed ignominiously in the attempt. She was a very faulty and passionately human child, with no aspirations toward being an angel of the house, but she had a sense of duty and a desire to be good,—respectably, decently good. Whenever she fell below this self-imposed standard she was miserable. She did not like to be under her aunt's roof, eating bread, wearing clothes, and studying books provided by her, and dislike her so heartily all the time. She felt instinctively that this was wrong and mean, and whenever the feeling of remorse was strong within her she made a desperate effort to please her grim and difficult relative. But how could she succeed when she was never herself in her Aunt Miranda's presence? The

searching look of the eyes, the sharp voice, the hard knotty fingers, the thin straight lips, the long silences, the "front-piece" that didn't match her hair, the very obvious "parting" that seemed sewed in with linen thread on black net—there was not a single item that appealed to Rebecca. There are certain narrow, unimaginative, and autocratic old people who seem to call out the most mischievous, and sometimes the worst traits in children. Miss Miranda, had she lived in a populous neighborhood, would have had her doorbell pulled, her gate tied up, or "dirt traps" set in her garden paths. The Simpson twins stood in such awe of her that they could not be persuaded to come to the side door even when Miss Jane held gingerbread cookies in her outstretched hands.

It is needless to say that Rebecca irritated her aunt with every breath she drew. She continually forgot and started up the front stairs because it was the shortest route to her bedroom; she left the dipper on the kitchen shelf instead of hanging it up over the pail; she sat in the chair the cat liked best; she was willing to go on errands, but often forgot what she was sent for; she left the screen doors ajar, so that flies came in; her tongue was ever in motion; she sang or whistled when she was picking up chips; she was always messing with flowers, putting them in vases, pinning them on her dress, and sticking them in her hat; finally she was an everlasting reminder of her foolish, worthless father, whose handsome face and engaging manner had so deceived Aurelia, and perhaps, if the facts were known, others besides Aurelia. The Randalls were aliens. They had not been born in Riverboro nor even in York County. Miranda would have allowed, on compulsion, that in the nature of things a large number of persons must necessarily be born outside this sacred precinct; but she had her opinion of them, and it was not a flattering one. Now if Hannah had come—Hannah took after the other side of the house; she was "all Sawyer." (Poor Hannah! that was true!) Hannah spoke only when spoken to, instead of first, last, and all the time; Hannah at fourteen was a member of the church; Hannah liked to knit; Hannah was, probably, or would have been, a pattern of all the smaller virtues; instead of which here was this black-haired gypsy, with eyes as big as cartwheels, installed as a member of the household.

What sunshine in a shady place was Aunt Jane to Rebecca! Aunt Jane with her quiet voice, her understanding eyes, her ready excuses, in these first difficult weeks, when the impulsive little stranger was trying to settle down into the "brick house ways." She did learn them, in part, and by degrees, and the constant fitting of herself to these new and difficult standards of conduct seemed to make her older than ever for her years.

The child took her sewing and sat beside Aunt Jane in the kitchen while Aunt Miranda had the post of observation at the sitting-room window. Sometimes they would work on the side porch where the clematis and woodbine shaded them from the hot sun. To Rebecca the lengths of brown gingham were interminable. She made hard work of sewing, broke the thread, dropped her thimble into the syringa bushes, pricked her finger, wiped the perspiration from her forehead, could not match the checks, puckered the seams. She polished her needles to nothing, pushing them in and out of the emery strawberry, but they always squeaked. Still Aunt Jane's patience held good, and some small measure of skill was creeping into Rebecca's fingers, fingers that held pencil, paint brush, and pen so cleverly and were so clumsy with the dainty little needle.

When the first brown gingham frock was completed, the child seized what she thought an opportune moment and asked her Aunt Miranda if she might have another color for the next one.

"I bought a whole piece of the brown," said Miranda laconically. "That'll give you two more dresses, with plenty for new sleeves, and to patch and let down with, an' be more economical."

"I know. But Mr. Watson says he'll take back part of it, and let us have pink and blue for the same price."

"Did you ask him?"

"Yes'm."

"It was none o' your business."

"I was helping Emma Jane choose aprons, and didn't think you'd mind which color I had. Pink keeps clean just as nice as brown, and Mr. Watson says it'll boil without fading."

"Mr. Watson's a splendid judge of washing, I guess. I don't approve of children being rigged out in fancy colors, but I'll see what your Aunt Jane thinks."

"I think it would be all right to let Rebecca have one pink and one blue gingham," said Jane. "A child gets tired of sewing on one color. It's only natural she should long for a change; besides she'd look like a charity child always wearing the same brown with a white apron. And it's dreadful unbecoming to her!"

" 'Handsome is as handsome does,' say I. Rebecca never'll come to grief along of her beauty, that's certain, and there's no use in humoring her to think about her looks.

I believe she's vain as a peacock now, without anything to be vain of."

"She's young and attracted to bright things—that's all. I remember well enough how I felt at her age."

"You was considerable of a fool at her age, Jane."

"Yes, I was, thank the Lord! I only wish I'd known how to take a little of my foolishness along with me, as some folks do, to brighten my declining years."

There finally was a pink gingham, and when it was nicely finished, Aunt Jane gave Rebecca a delightful surprise. She showed her how to make a pretty trimming of narrow white linen tape, by folding it in pointed shapes and sewing it down very flat with neat little stitches.

"It'll be good fancy work for you, Rebecca; for your Aunt Miranda won't like to see you always reading in the long winter evenings. Now if you think you can baste two rows of white tape round the bottom of your pink skirt and keep it straight by the checks, I'll stitch them on for you and trim the waist and sleeves with pointed tape-trimming, so the dress'll be really pretty for second-best."

Rebecca's joy knew no bounds. "I'll baste like a house afire!" she exclaimed. "It's a thousand yards round that skirt, as well I know, having hemmed it; but I could sew pretty trimming on if it was from here to Milltown. Oh! do you think Aunt Mirandy'll ever let me go to Milltown with Mr. Cobb? He's asked me again, you know; but one Saturday I had to pick strawberries, and another it rained, and I don't think she really approves of my going. It's *twenty-nine* minutes past four, Aunt Jane, and Alice Robinson has been sitting under the currant bushes for a long time waiting for me. Can I go and play?"

"Yes, you may go, and you'd better run as far as you can out behind the barn, so 't your noise won't distract your Aunt Mirandy. I see Susan Simpson and the twins and Emma Jane Perkins hiding behind the fence."

Rebecca leaped off the porch, snatched Alice Robinson from under the currant bushes, and what was much more difficult, succeeded by means of a complicated system of signals, in getting Emma Jane away from the Simpson party and giving them the slip altogether. They were much too small for certain pleasurable activities planned for that afternoon; but they were not to be despised, for they had the most fascinating dooryard in the village. In it, in bewildering confusion, were old sleighs, pungs, horse rakes, hogsheads, settees without backs, bedsteads without heads, in all stages of disability, and never the same on two consecutive days. Mrs. Simpson was seldom at home, and even when she was, had little concern as to what happened on the premises. A favorite diversion was to make the house into a fort, gallantly held by a handful of American soldiers against a besieging force of the British army. Great care was used in apportioning the parts, for there was no disposition to let anybody win but the Americans. Seesaw Simpson was usually made commander-in-chief of the British army, and a limp and uncertain one he was, capable, with his contradictory orders and his fondness for the extreme rear, of leading any regiment to an inglorious death. Sometimes the long-suffering house was a log hut, and the brave settlers defeated a band of hostile Indians, or occasionally were massacred by them; but in either case the Simpson house looked, to quote a Riverboro expression, "as if the devil had been having an auction in it."

Chapter Six

Color of Rose

On the very next Friday there were great doings in the little schoolhouse on the hill. Friday afternoon was always the time chosen for dialogues, songs, and recitations, but it cannot be stated that it was a gala day in any true sense of the word. Most of the children hated "speaking pieces"; hated the burden of learning them, dreaded the danger of breaking down in them. Miss Dearborn commonly went home with a headache, and never left her bed during the rest of the afternoon or evening; and the casual female parent who attended the exercises sat on a front bench with beads of cold sweat on her forehead, listening to the all-too-familiar halts and stammers. Sometimes a bellowing infant who had clean forgotten his verse would cast himself bodily on the maternal bosom and be borne out into the open air, where he was sometimes kissed and occasionally spanked; but in any case the failure added an extra dash of gloom and dread to the occasion. The advent of Rebecca had somehow infused a new spirit into these hitherto terrible afternoons. She had taught Elijah and Elisha Simpson so that they recited three verses of something with such comical effect that they delighted themselves, the teacher, and the school; while Susan, who lisped, had been provided with a humorous poem in which she impersonated a lisping child. Emma Jane and Rebecca had a dialogue, and the sense of companionship buoyed up Emma Jane and gave her self-reliance. In fact, Miss Dearborn announced on this particular Friday morning that the exercises promised to be so interesting that she had invited the doctor's wife, the minister's wife, two members of the school committee, and a few mothers. Living Perkins was asked to decorate one of the blackboards and Rebecca the other. Living, who was the star artist of the school, chose the map of North America. Rebecca liked better to draw things less realistic, and speedily, before the eyes of the enchanted multitude, there grew under her skillful fingers an American flag done in red, white, and blue chalk, every star in its right place, every stripe fluttering in the breeze. Beside this appeared a figure of Columbia, copied from the top of the cigar box that held the crayons.

Miss Dearborn was delighted. "I propose we give Rebecca a good hand-clapping for such a beautiful picture—one that the whole school may well be proud of!"

The scholars clapped heartily, and Dick Carter, leaping to his feet, waved his hand and gave a rousing cheer.

Rebecca's heart leaped for joy, and to her confusion she felt the tears rising in her eyes. She could hardly see the way back to her seat, for in her ignorant lonely little life she had never been singled out for applause, never lauded, nor crowned, as in this wonderful, dazzling moment. If "nobleness enkindleth nobleness," so does enthusiasm beget enthusiasm, and so do wit and talent enkindle wit and talent. Alice Robinson proposed that the school should sing "Three Cheers for the Red, White, and Blue!" and when they came to the chorus, all point to Rebecca's flag. Dick Carter suggested that Living Perkins and Rebecca Randall should sign their names to their pictures, so that the visitors would, know who drew them. Huldah Meserve asked permission to cover the largest holes in the plastered walls with boughs and fill the water pail with wild flowers. Rebecca's mood was above and beyond all practical details. She sat silent, her heart so full of grateful joy that she could hardly remember the words of her dialogue. At recess she bore herself modestly, notwithstanding her great triumph. Minnie Smellie gathered maple boughs and covered the ugly stove with them, under Rebecca's direction.

Miss Dearborn dismissed the morning session at quarter to twelve, so that those who lived near enough could go home for a change of dress. Emma Jane and Rebecca ran nearly every step of the way, from sheer excitement, only stopping to breathe at the stiles.

"Will your Aunt Mirandy let you wear your best, or only your buff calico?" asked Emma Jane.

"I think I'll ask Aunt Jane," Rebecca replied. "Oh! if my pink was only finished! I left Aunt Jane making the button-holes!"

"I'm going to ask my mother to let me wear her garnet ring," said Emma Jane. "It would look perfectly elergant flashing in the sun when I point to the flag. Good-bye; don't wait for me going back; I may get a ride."

Rebecca found the side door locked, but she knew that

the key was under the step, and so of course did everybody else in Riverboro, for they all did about the same thing with it. She unlocked the door and went into the dining-room to find her lunch laid on the table and a note from Aunt Jane saying that they had gone to Moderation with Mrs. Robinson in her carryall. Rebecca swallowed a piece of bread and butter, and flew up the front stairs to her bedroom. On the bed lay the pink gingham dress finished by Aunt Jane's kind hands. Could she, dare she, wear it without asking? Did the occasion justify a new costume, or would her aunts think she ought to keep it for the concert?

"I'll wear it," thought Rebecca. "They're not here to ask, and maybe they wouldn't mind a bit; it's only gingham after all, and wouldn't be so grand if it wasn't new, and hadn't tape trimming on it, and wasn't pink."

She unbraided her two pigtails, combed out the waves of her hair and tied them back with a ribbon, changed her shoes, and then slipped on the pretty frock, managing to fasten all but the three middle buttons, which she reserved for Emma Jane.

Then her eye fell on her cherished pink sunshade, the exact match, and the girls had never seen it. It wasn't quite appropriate for school, but she needn't take it into the room; she would wrap it in a piece of paper, just show it, and carry it coming home. She glanced in the parlor looking-glass downstairs and was electrified at the vision. It seemed almost as if beauty of apparel could go no further than that heavenly pink gingham dress! The sparkle of her eyes, glow of her cheeks, sheen of her falling hair, passed unnoticed in the all-conquering charm of the rose-colored garment.

Goodness! it was twenty minutes to one and she would be late. She danced out the side door, pulled a pink rose from a bush at the gate, and covered the mile between the brick house and the seat of learning in an incredibly short time, meeting Emma Jane, also breathless and resplendent, at the entrance.

"Rebecca Randall!" exclaimed Emma Jane, "you're handsome as a picture!"

"I?" laughed Rebecca. "Nonsense! it's only the pink gingham."

"You're not good looking every day," insisted Emma Jane; "but you're different somehow. See my garnet ring; Mother scrubbed it in soap and water. How on earth did your Aunt Mirandy let you put on your bran' new dress?"

"They were both away and I didn't ask," Rebecca responded anxiously. "Why? Do you think they'd have said no?"

"Miss Mirandy always says no, doesn't she?" asked Emma Jane.

"Ye—es; but this afternoon is very special—almost like a Sunday-School concert."

"Yes," assented Emma Jane, "it is, of course; with your name on the board, and our pointing to your flag, and our elergant dialogue, and all that."

The afternoon was one succession of solid triumphs for everybody concerned. There were no real failures at all, no tears, no parents ashamed of their offspring. Miss Dearborn heard many admiring remarks passed upon her ability, and wondered whether they belonged to her or partly, at least, to Rebecca. The child had no more to do than several others, but she was somehow in the foreground. It transpired afterwards at various village entertainments that Rebecca couldn't be kept in the background; it positively refused to hold her. Her worst enemy could not have called her pushing. She was ready and willing and never shy; but she sought for no chances of display and was, indeed, remarkably lacking in self-consciousness, as well as eager to bring others into whatever fun or entertainment there was. If wherever the MacGregor sat was the head of the table, so in the same way wherever Rebecca stood was the center of the stage. Her clear high treble soared above all the rest in the choruses, and somehow everybody watched her, took note of her gestures, her whole-souled singing, her irrepressible enthusiasm.

Finally it was all over, and it seemed to Rebecca as if she should never be cool and calm again, as she loitered on the homeward path. There would be no lessons to learn to-night, and the vision of helping with the preserves on the morrow had no terrors for her—fears could not draw breath in the radiance that flooded her soul. There were thick gathering clouds in the sky, but she took no note of them save to be glad that she could raise her sunshade. She did not tread the solid ground at all, or have any sense of belonging to the common human family, until she entered the side yard of the brick house and saw her Aunt Miranda standing in the open doorway. Then with a rush she came back to earth.

Chapter Seven

Ashes of Roses

There she is, over an hour late; a little more an' she'd 'a' been caught in a thunder shower, but she'd never look ahead," said Miranda to Jane; "and added to all her other iniquities, if she ain't rigged out in that new dress, steppin' along with her father's dancin'-school steps, and swingin' her parasol for all the world as if she was play-actin'. Now I'm the oldest, Jane, an' I intend to have my say out; if you don't like it you can go into the kitchen till it's over. Step right in here, Rebecca; I want to talk to you. What did you put on that good new dress for, on a school day, without permission?"

"I had intended to ask you at noontime, but you weren't at home, so I couldn't," began Rebecca.

"You did no such a thing; you put it on because you was left alone, though you knew well enough I wouldn't have let you."

"If I'd been *certain* you wouldn't have let me I'd never have done it," said Rebecca, trying to be truthful; "but I wasn't *certain*, and it was worth risking. I thought perhaps you might, if you knew it was almost a real exhibition at school."

"Exhibition!" exclaimed Miranda scornfully; "you are exhibition enough by yourself, I should say. Was you exhibitin' your parasol?"

"The parasol *was* silly," confessed Rebecca, hanging her head; "but it's the only time in my whole life when I had anything to match it, and it looked so beautiful with the pink dress! Emma Jane and I spoke a dialogue about a city girl and a country girl, and it came to me just the minute before I started how nice it would come in for the city girl; and it did. I haven't hurt my dress a mite, Aunt Mirandy."

"It's the craftiness and underhandedness of your actions that's the worst," said Miranda coldly. "And look at the other things you've done! It seems as if Satan possessed you! You went up the front stairs to your room, but you didn't hide your tracks, for you dropped your handkerchief on the way up. You left the screen out of your bedroom window for the flies to come in all over the house. You never cleared away your lunch nor set away a dish, *and you left the side door unlocked* from half-past twelve to three o'clock, so 't anybody could 'a' come in and stolen what they liked!"

Rebecca sat down heavily in her chair as she heard the list of her transgressions. How could she have been so careless? The tears began to flow now as she attempted to explain sins that never could be explained or justified.

"Oh, I'm so sorry!" she faltered. "I was trimming the schoolroom, and got belated, and ran all the way home. It was hard getting into my dress alone, and I hadn't time to eat but a mouthful, and just at the last minute, when I honestly—*honestly*—would have thought about clearing away and locking up, I looked at the clock and knew I could hardly get back to school in time to form in the line; and I thought how dreadful it would be to go in late and get my first black mark on a Friday afternoon, with the minister's wife and the doctor's wife and the school committee all there!"

"Don't wail and carry on now; it's no good cryin' over spilt milk," answered Miranda. "An ounce of good behavior is worth a pound of repentance. Instead of tryin' to see how little trouble you can make in a house that ain't your own home, it seems as if you tried to see how much you could put us out. Take that rose out o' your dress and let me see the spot it's made on your yoke, an' the rust holes where the wet pin went in. No, it ain't; but it's more by luck than forethought. I ain't got any patience with your flowers and frizzled-out hair and furbelows an' airs an' graces, for all the world like your Miss-Nancy father."

Rebecca lifted her head in a flash. "Look here, Aunt Mirandy, I'll be as good as I know how to be. I'll mind quick when I'm spoken to and never leave the door unlocked again, but I won't have my father called names. He was a p-perfectly l-lovely father, that's what he was, and it's *mean* to call him Miss Nancy!"

"Don't you dare answer me back that imperdent way, Rebecca, tellin' me I'm mean; your father was a vain, foolish, shiftless man, an' you might as well hear it from me as anybody else; he spent your mother's money and left her with seven children to provide for."

"It's s-something to leave s-seven nice children," sobbed Rebecca.

"Not when other folks have to help feed, clothe, and educate 'em," responded Miranda. "Now you step upstairs, put on your nightgown, go to bed, and stay there till mornin'. You'll find a bowl o' crackers an' milk on your bureau, an' I don't want to hear a sound from you till breakfast time. Jane, run an' take the dish towels off the line and shut the shed doors; we're goin' to have a turrible shower."

"We've had it, I should think," said Jane quietly, as she went to do her sister's bidding. "I don't often speak my mind, Mirandy; but you ought not to have said what you did about Lorenzo. He was what he was, and can't be made any different; but he was Rebecca's father, and Aurelia always says he was a good husband."

Miranda had never heard the proverbial phrase about the only "good Indian," but her mind worked in the conventional manner when she said grimly, "Yes, I've noticed that dead husbands are usually good ones; but the truth needs an airin' now and then, and that child will never amount to a hill o' beans till she gets some of her father trounced out of her. I'm glad I said just what I did."

"I dare say you are," remarked Jane, with what might be described as one of her annual bursts of courage; "but all the same, Mirandy, it wasn't good manners, and it wasn't good religion!"

The clap of thunder that shook the house just at that moment made no such peal in Miranda Sawyer's ears as Jane's remark made when it fell with a deafening roar on her conscience.

Perhaps after all it is just as well to speak only once a year and then speak to the purpose.

Rebecca mounted the back stairs wearily, closed the door

of her bedroom, and took off the beloved pink gingham with trembling fingers. Her cotton handkerchief was rolled into a hard ball, and in the intervals of reaching the more difficult buttons that lay between her shoulder blades and her belt, she dabbed her wet eyes carefully, so that they should not rain salt water on the finery that had been worn at such a price. She smoothed it out carefully, pinched up the white ruffle at the neck, and laid it away in a drawer with an extra little sob at the roughness of life. The withered pink rose fell on the floor. Rebecca looked at it and thought to herself, "Just like my happy day!" Nothing could show more clearly the kind of child she was than the fact that she instantly perceived the symbolism of the rose, and laid it in the drawer with the dress as if she were burying the whole episode with all its sad memories. It was a child's poetic instinct with a dawning hint of woman's sentiment in it.

She braided her hair in the two accustomed pigtails, took off her best shoes (which had happily escaped notice), with all the while a fixed resolve growing in her mind, that of leaving the brick house and going back to the farm. She would not be received there with open arms,—there was no hope of that,—but she would help her mother about the house and send Hannah to Riverboro in her place. "I hope she'll like it!" she thought in a momentary burst of vindictiveness. She sat by the window trying to make some sort of plan, watching the lightning play over the hilltop and the streams of rain chasing each other down the lightning rod. And this was the day that had dawned so joyfully! It had been a red sunrise, and she had leaned on the window sill studying her lesson and thinking what a lovely world it

was. And what a golden morning! The changing of the
bare, ugly little schoolroom into a bower of beauty; Miss
Dearborn's pleasure at her success with the Simpson twins'
recitation; the privilege of decorating the blackboard; the
happy thought of drawing Columbia from the cigar box; the
intoxicating moment when the school clapped her! And
what an afternoon! How it went on from glory to glory, beginning with Emma Jane's telling her, Rebecca Randall, that
she was as "handsome as a picture."

She lived through the exercises again in memory, especially her dialogue with Emma Jane and her inspiration of
using the bough-covered stove as a mossy bank where the
country girl could sit and watch her flocks. This gave Emma
Jane a feeling of such ease that she never recited better; and
how generous it was of her to lend the garnet ring to the
city girl, fancying truly how it would flash as she furled her
parasol and approached the awe-stricken shepherdess! She
had thought Aunt Miranda might be pleased that the niece
invited down from the farm had succeeded so well at school;
but no, there was no hope of pleasing her in that or in any
other way. She would go to Maplewood on the stage next
day with Mr. Cobb and get home somehow from cousin
Ann's. On second thoughts her aunts might not allow it.
Very well, she would slip away now and see if she could
stay all night with the Cobbs and be off next morning before
breakfast.

Rebecca never stopped long to think, more's the pity, so
she put on her oldest dress and hat and jacket, then wrapped
her nightdress, comb, and toothbrush in a bundle and
dropped it softly out of the window. Her room was in the L
and her window at no very dangerous distance from the

ground, though had it been, nothing could have stopped her at that moment. Somebody who had gone on the roof to clean out the gutters had left a cleat nailed to the side of the house about halfway between the window and the top of the back porch. Rebecca heard the sound of the sewing machine in the dining-room and the chopping of meat in the kitchen; so knowing the whereabouts of both her aunts, she scrambled out of the window, caught hold of the lightning rod, slid down to the helpful cleat, jumped to the porch, used the woodbine trellis for a ladder, and was flying up the road in the storm before she had time to arrange any details of her future movements.

Jeremiah Cobb sat at his lonely supper at the table by the kitchen window. "Mother," as he with his old-fashioned habits was in the habit of calling his wife, was nursing a sick neighbor. Mrs. Cobb was mother only to a little headstone in the churchyard, where reposed "Sarah Ann, beloved daughter of Jeremiah and Sarah Cobb, aged seventeen months"; but the name of mother was better than nothing, and served at any rate as a reminder of her woman's crown of blessedness.

The rain still fell, and the heavens were dark, though it was scarcely five o'clock. Looking up from his "dish of tea," the old man saw at the open door a very figure of woe. Rebecca's face was so swollen with tears and so sharp with misery that for a moment he scarcely recognized her. Then when he heard her voice asking, "Please may I come in, Mr. Cobb?" he cried, "Well, I vow! It's my little lady passenger! Come to call on old Uncle Jerry and pass the time o' day, hev ye? Why, you're wet as sops. Draw up to the stove. I made a fire, hot as it was, thinkin' I wanted somethin' warm

for my supper, bein' kind o' lonesome without mother.
She's settin' up with Seth Strout to-night. There, we'll hang
your soppy hat on the nail, put your jacket over the chair
rail, an' then you turn your back to the stove an' dry yourself good."

Uncle Jerry had never before said so many words at a
time, but he had caught sight of the child's red eyes and
tear-stained cheeks, and his big heart went out to her in her
trouble, quite regardless of any circumstances that might
have caused it.

Rebecca stood still for a moment until Uncle Jerry took
his seat again at the table, and then, unable to contain herself longer, cried, "Oh, Mr. Cobb, I've run away from the
brick house, and I want to go back to the farm. Will you
keep me to-night and take me up to Maplewood in the stage?
I haven't got any money for my fare, but I'll earn it somehow
afterwards."

"Well, I guess we won't quarrel 'bout money, you and
me," said the old man; "and we've never had our ride together, anyway, though we allers meant to go down river,
not up."

"I shall never see Milltown now!" sobbed Rebecca.

"Come over here side o' me an' tell me all about it,"
coaxed Uncle Jerry. "Jest set down on that there wooden
cricket an' out with the whole story."

Rebecca leaned her aching head against Mr. Cobb's
homespun knee and recounted the history of her trouble.
Tragic as that history seemed to her passionate and undis-
ciplined mind, she told it truthfully and without exaggera-
tion.

Chapter Eight

Rainbow Bridges

Uncle Jerry coughed and stirred in his chair a good deal during Rebecca's recital, but he carefully concealed any undue feeling of sympathy, just muttering, "Poor little soul! We'll see what we can do for her!"

"You will take me to Maplewood, won't you, Mr. Cobb?" begged Rebecca piteously.

"Don't you fret a mite," he answered, with a crafty little notion at the back of his mind; "I'll see the lady passenger through somehow. Now take a bite o' somethin' to eat, child. Spread some o' that tomato preserve on your bread; draw up to the table. How'd you like to set in Mother's place an' pour me out another cup o' hot tea?"

Mr. Jeremiah Cobb's mental machinery was simple, and did not move very smoothly save when propelled by his affection or sympathy. In the present case these were both employed to his advantage, and mourning his stupidity and praying for some flash of inspiration to light his path, he blundered along, trusting to Providence.

Rebecca, comforted by the old man's tone, and timidly

enjoying the dignity of sitting in Mrs. Cobb's seat and lifting the blue china teapot, smiled faintly, smoothed her hair, and dried her eyes.

"I suppose your mother'll be turrible glad to see you back again?" queried Mr. Cobb.

A tiny fear—just a baby thing—in the bottom of Rebecca's heart stirred and grew larger the moment it was touched with a question.

"She won't like it that I ran away, I s'pose, and she'll be sorry that I couldn't please Aunt Mirandy; but I'll make her understand, just as I did you."

"I s'pose she was thinkin' o' your schoolin', lettin' you come down here; but land! you can go to school in Temperance, I s'pose?"

"There's only two months' school now in Temperance, and the farm's too far from all the other schools."

"Oh, well! there's other things in the world beside edjercation," responded Uncle Jerry, attacking a piece of apple pie.

"Ye—es; though Mother thought that was going to be the making of me," returned Rebecca sadly, giving a dry little sob as she tried to drink her tea.

"It'll be nice for you to be all together again at the farm—such a house full o' children!" remarked the dear old deceiver, who longed for nothing so much as to cuddle and comfort the poor little creature.

"It's too full—that's the trouble. But I'll make Hannah come to Riverboro in my place."

"S'pose Mirandy 'n' Jane'll have her? I should be 'most

afraid they wouldn't. They'll be kind o' mad at your goin' home, you know, and you can't hardly blame 'em."

This was quite a new thought,—that the brick house might be closed to Hannah, since she, Rebecca, had turned her back upon its cold hospitality.

"How is this school down here in Riverboro—pretty good?" inquired Uncle Jerry, whose brain was working with an altogether unaccustomed rapidity,—so much so that it almost terrified him.

"Oh, it's a splendid school! And Miss Dearborn is a splendid teacher!"

"You like her, do you? Well, you'd better believe she returns the compliment. Mother was down to the store this afternoon buyin' liniment for Seth Strout an' she met Miss Dearborn on the bridge. They got to talkin' 'bout school, for mother has summer-boarded a lot o' the schoolmarms, an' likes 'em. 'How does the little Temperance girl git along?' asks Mother. 'Oh, she's the best scholar I have!' says Miss Dearborn. 'I could teach school from sunup to sundown if scholars was all like Rebecca Randall,' says she."

"Oh, Mr. Cobb, *did* she say that?" glowed Rebecca, her face sparkling and dimpling in an instant. "I've tried hard all the time, but I'll study the covers right off of the books now."

"You mean you would if you'd ben goin' to stay here," interposed Uncle Jerry. "Now ain't it too bad you've jest got to give it all up on account o' your Aunt Mirandy? Well, I can't hardly blame ye. She's cranky an' she's sour; I should think she'd ben nussed on bonny-clabber an' green apples.

She needs bearin' with; an' I guess you ain't much on patience, be ye?"

"Not very much," replied Rebecca dolefully.

"If I'd had this talk with ye yesterday," pursued Mr.
Cobb, "I believe I'd have advised ye different. It's too late
now, an' I don't feel to say you've ben all in the wrong; but
if 't was to do over again, I'd say, well, your Aunt Mirandy
gives you clothes and board and schoolin' and is goin' to
send you to Wareham at a big expense. She's turrible hard
to get along with, an' kind o' heaves benefits at your head,
same's she would bricks; but they're benefits jest the same,
an' mebbe it's your job to kind o' pay for 'em in good behavior. Jane's a leetle bit more easy-goin' than Mirandy,
ain't she, or is she jest as hard to please?"

"Oh, Aunt Jane and I get along splendidly," exclaimed
Rebecca; "she's just as good and kind as she can be, and I
like her better all the time. I think she kind of likes me, too;
she smoothed my hair once. I'd let her scold me all day
long, for she understands; but she can't stand up for me
against Aunt Mirandy; she's about as afraid of her as I am."

"Jane'll be real sorry to-morrow to find you've gone away,
I guess; but never mind, it can't be helped. If she has a kind
of a dull time with Mirandy, on account o' her bein' so
sharp, why of course she'd set great store by your comp'ny.
Mother was talkin' with her after prayer meetin' the other
night. 'You wouldn't know the brick house, Sarah,' says
Jane. 'I'm keepin' a sewin' school, an' my scholar has made
three dresses. What do you think o' that,' says she, 'for an
old maid's child? I've taken a class in Sunday-School,' says

Jane, 'an' think o' renewin' my youth an' goin' to the picnic with Rebecca,' says she; an' Mother declares she never see her look so young 'n' happy."

There was a silence that could be felt in the little kitchen; a silence only broken by the ticking of the tall clock and the beating of Rebecca's heart, which, it seemed to her, almost drowned the voice of the clock. The rain ceased, a sudden rosy light filled the room, and through the window a rainbow could be seen spanning the heavens like a radiant bridge. Bridges took one across difficult places, thought Rebecca, and Uncle Jerry seemed to have built one over her troubles and given her strength to walk.

"The shower's over," said the old man, filling his pipe; "it's cleared the air, washed the face o' the airth nice an' clean, an' everything to-morrer will shine like a new pin— when you an' I are drivin' up river."

Rebecca pushed her cup away, rose from the table, and put on her hat and jacket quietly. "I'm not going to drive up river, Mr. Cobb," she said. "I'm going to stay here and —catch bricks; catch 'em without throwing 'em back, too. I don't know as Aunt Mirandy will take me in after I've run away, but I'm going back now while I have the courage. You wouldn't be so good as to go with me, would you, Mr. Cobb?"

"You'd better b'lieve your Uncle Jerry don't propose to leave till he gits this thing fixed up," cried the old man delightedly. "Now you've had all you can stan' to-night, poor little soul, without gettin' a fit o' sickness; an' Mirandy'll be sore an' cross an' in no condition for argyment;

so my plan is jest this: to drive you over to the brick house in
my top buggy; to have you set back in the corner, an' I git
out an' go to the side door; an' when I git your Aunt Mirandy 'n' Aunt Jane out int' the shed to plan for a load o'
wood I'm goin' to have hauled there this week, you'll slip
out o' the buggy and go upstairs to bed. The front door
won't be locked, will it?"

"Not this time of night," Rebecca answered; "not till Aunt
Mirandy goes to bed; but oh! what if it should be?"

"Well, it won't; an' if 't is, why we'll have to face it out;
though in my opinion there's things that won't bear facin'
out an' had better be settled comfortable an' quiet. You
see you ain't run away yet; you've only come over here to
consult me 'bout runnin' away, an' we've concluded it ain't
wuth the trouble. The only real sin you've committed, as I
figger it out, was in comin' here by the winder when you'd
ben sent to bed. That ain't so very black, an' you can tell
your Aunt Jane 'bout it come Sunday, when she's chock full
o' religion, an' she can advise you when you'd better tell
your Aunt Mirandy. I don't believe in deceivin' folks, but if
you've hed hard thoughts you ain't obleeged to own 'em up;
take 'em to the Lord in prayer, as the hymn says, and then
don't go on hevin' 'em. Now come on; I'm all hitched up to
go over to the post-office; don't forget your bundle; 'it's always a journey, Mother, when you carry a nightgown';
them's the first words your Uncle Jerry ever heard you say!
He didn't think you'd be bringin' your nightgown over to
his house. Step in an' curl up in the corner; we ain't goin' to
let folks see little runaway gals, 'cause they're goin' back to
begin all over ag'in!"

When Rebecca crept upstairs, and undressing in the dark finally found herself in her bed that night, though she was aching and throbbing in every nerve, she felt a kind of peace stealing over her. She had been saved from foolishness and error; kept from troubling her poor mother; prevented from angering and mortifying her aunts.

Her heart was melted now, and she determined to win Aunt Miranda's approval by some desperate means, and to try and forget the one thing that rankled worst, the scornful mention of her father, of whom she thought with the greatest admiration, and whom she had not yet heard criticized; for such sorrows and disappointments as Aurelia Randall had suffered had never been communicated to her children.

It would have been some comfort to the bruised, unhappy little spirit to know that Miranda Sawyer was passing an uncomfortable night, and that she tacitly regretted her harshness, partly because Jane had taken such a lofty and virtuous position in the matter. She could not endure Jane's disapproval, although she would never have confessed to such a weakness.

As Uncle Jerry drove homeward under the stars, well content with his attempts at keeping the peace, he thought wistfully of the touch of Rebecca's head on his knee, and the rain of her tears on his hand; of the sweet reasonableness of her mind when she had the matter put rightly before her; of her quick decision when she had once seen the path of duty; of the touching hunger for love and understanding that were so characteristic in her. "Lord A'mighty!" he ejaculated under his breath, "Lord A'mighty! to hector and

abuse a child like that one! 'Tain't *abuse* exactly, I know, or
't wouldn't be to some o' your elephant-hided young ones;
but to that little tender will-o'-the-wisp a hard word's like a
lash. Mirandy Sawyer would be a heap better woman if she
had a little gravestun to remember, same's Mother 'n' I
have."

"I never see a child improve in her work as Rebecca has
to-day," remarked Miranda Sawyer to Jane on Saturday
evening. "That settin' down I gave her was probably just
what she needed, and I dare say it'll last for a month."

"I'm glad you're pleased," returned Jane. "A cringing
worm is what you want, not a bright, smiling child. Rebecca looks to me as if she'd been through the Seven Years'
War. When she came downstairs this morning it seemed to
me she'd grown old in the night. If you follow my advice,
which you seldom do, you'll let me take her and Emma Jane
down beside the river to-morrow afternoon and bring Emma
Jane home to a good Sunday supper. Then if you'll let her
go to Milltown with the Cobbs on Wednesday, that'll
hearten her up a little and coax back her appetite. Wednesday's a holiday on account of Miss Dearborn's going home
to her sister's wedding, and the Cobbs and Perkinses want
to go down to the Agricultural Fair."

Chapter Nine

"The Stirring of the Powers"

Rebecca's visit to Milltown was all that her glowing fancy had painted it, except that recent readings about Rome and Venice disposed her to believe that those cities might have an advantage over Milltown in the matter of mere pictorial beauty. So soon does the soul outgrow its mansions that after once seeing Milltown her fancy ran out to the future sight of Portland; for that, having islands and a harbor and two public monuments, must be far more beautiful than Milltown, which would, she felt, take its proud place among the cities of the earth, by reason of its tremendous business activity rather than by any irresistible appeal to the imagination.

It would be impossible for two children to see more, do more, walk more, talk more, eat more, or ask more questions than Rebecca and Emma Jane did on that eventful Wednesday.

"She's the best company I ever see in all my life," said Mrs. Cobb to her husband that evening. "We ain't had a dull minute this day. She's well-mannered, too; she didn't ask for anything, and was thankful for whatever she got. Did you watch her face when we went into that tent where they was actin' out 'Uncle Tom's Cabin'? And did you take notice of the way she told us about the book when we sat down to have our ice cream? I tell you Harriet Beecher Stowe herself couldn't 'a' done it better justice."

"I took it all in," responded Mr. Cobb, who was pleased that "mother" agreed with him about Rebecca. "I ain't sure but she's goin' to turn out somethin' remarkable,—a singer, or a writer, or a lady doctor like that Miss Parks up to Cornish."

"I can't see Rebecca as a lady doctor, somehow," mused Mrs. Cobb. "Her gift o' gab is what's goin' to be the makin' of her; mebbe she'll lecture, or recite pieces, like that Portland elocutionist that come out here to the harvest supper."

"I guess she'll be able to write down her own pieces," said Mr. Cobb confidently; "she could make 'em up faster'n she could read 'em out of a book."

"It's a pity she's so plain looking," remarked Mrs. Cobb, blowing out the candle.

"*Plain looking*, Mother?" exclaimed her husband in astonishment. "Look at the eyes of her; look at the hair of her, an' the smile, an' that there dimple! Look at Alice Robinson, that's called the prettiest child on the river, an' see how Rebecca shines her ri' down out o' sight! I hope Mirandy'll favor her comin' over to see us real often, for she'll let off some of her steam here, an' the brick house'll be consid'able safer for everybody concerned. We've known what it was to hev children, even if 't was more'n thirty years ago, an' we can make allowances."

Notwithstanding the encomiums of Mr. and Mrs. Cobb, Rebecca made a poor hand at composition writing at this time. Miss Dearborn gave her every sort of subject that she had ever been given herself: "Cloud Pictures"; "Abraham Lincoln"; "Nature"; "Philanthropy"; "Slavery"; "Intemperance"; "Joy and Duty"; "Solitude"; but with none of them did Rebecca seem to grapple satisfactorily.

"Write as you talk, Rebecca," insisted poor Miss Dearborn, who secretly knew that she could never manage a good composition herself.

"But gracious me, Miss Dearborn! I don't talk about nature and slavery. I can't write unless I have something to say, can I?"

"That is what compositions are for," returned Miss Dearborn doubtfully; "to make you have things to say. Now in your last one, on solitude, you haven't said anything very interesting, and you've made it too common and every-day to sound well. There are too many 'yous' and 'yours' in it; you ought to say 'one' now and then, to make it seem more like good writing. 'One opens a favorite book'; 'One's thoughts are a great comfort in solitude'; and so on."

"I don't know any more about solitude this week than I did about joy and duty last week," grumbled Rebecca.

"You tried to be funny about joy and duty," said Miss Dearborn reprovingly; "so of course you didn't succeed."

"I didn't know you were going to make us read the things out loud," said Rebecca with an embarrassed smile of recollection.

"Joy and Duty" had been the inspiring subject given to the older children for a theme to be written in five minutes.

Rebecca had wrestled, struggled, perspired in vain. When her turn came to read she was obliged to confess she had written nothing.

"You have at least two lines, Rebecca," insisted the teacher, "for I see them on your slate."

"I'd rather not read them, please; they are not good," pleaded Rebecca.

"Read what you have, good or bad, little or much; I am excusing nobody."

Rebecca rose, overcome with secret laughter, dread, and mortification; then in a low voice she read the couplet:—

> When Joy and Duty clash
> Let Duty go to smash.

Dick Carter's head disappeared under the desk, while Living Perkins choked with laughter.

Miss Dearborn laughed too.

"You must stay after school and try again, Rebecca," she said, but she said it smilingly. "Your poetry hasn't a very nice idea in it for a good little girl who ought to love duty."

"It wasn't *my* idea," said Rebecca apologetically. "I had only made the first line when I saw you were going to ring the bell and say the time was up. I had 'clash' written, and I couldn't think of anything then but 'hash' or 'rash' or 'smash.' I'll change it to this:—

> When Joy and Duty clash,
> 'T is Joy must go to smash."

"That is better," Miss Dearborn answered, "though I cannot think 'going to smash' is a pretty expression for poetry."

Having been instructed in the use of the indefinite pronoun "one" as giving a refined and elegant touch to literary efforts, Rebecca painstakingly rewrote her composition on solitude, giving it all the benefit of Miss Dearborn's suggestion. It then appeared in the following form, which hardly satisfied either teacher or pupil:—

SOLITUDE

It would be false to say that one could ever be alone when one has one's lovely thoughts to comfort one. One sits by one's self, it is true, but one thinks; one opens one's favorite book and reads one's favorite story; one speaks to one's aunt or one's brother, fondles one's cat, or looks at one's photograph album. There is one's work also: what a joy it is to one, if one happens to like work. All one's little household tasks keep one from being lonely. Does one ever feel bereft when one picks up one's chips to light one's fire for one's evening meal? Or when one washes one's milk pail before milking one's cow? One would fancy not.

R. R. R.

"It is perfectly dreadful," sighed Rebecca when she read it aloud after school. "Putting in 'one' all the time doesn't make it sound any more like a book, and it looks silly besides."

"You say such queer things," objected Miss Dearborn. "I don't see what makes you do it. Why did you put in anything so common as picking up chips?"

"Because I was talking about 'household tasks' in the sentence before, and it *is* one of my household tasks. Don't you think calling supper 'one's evening meal' is pretty? And isn't 'bereft' a nice word?"

"Yes, that part of it does very well. It is the cat, the chips, and the milk pail that I don't like."

"All right!" sighed Rebecca. "Out they go! Does the cow go too?"

"Yes, I don't like a cow in a composition," said the difficult Miss Dearborn.

The Milltown trip had not been without its tragic consequences of a small sort; for the next week Minnie Smellie's mother told Miranda Sawyer that she'd better look after Rebecca, for she was given to "swearing and profane language"; that she had been heard saying something dreadful that very afternoon, saying it before Emma Jane and Living Perkins, who only laughed and got down on all fours and chased her.

Rebecca, on being confronted and charged with the crime, denied it indignantly, and Aunt Jane believed her.

"Search your memory, Rebecca, and try to think what Minnie overheard you say," she pleaded. "Don't be ugly and obstinate, but think real hard. When did they chase you up the road, and what were you doing?"

A sudden light broke upon Rebecca's darkness.

"Oh! I see it now," she exclaimed. "It had rained hard all the morning, you know, and the road was full of puddles. Emma Jane, Living, and I were walking along, and I was ahead. I saw the water streaming over the road towards the ditch, and it reminded me of 'Uncle Tom's Cabin' at Milltown, when Eliza took her baby and ran across the Mississippi on the ice blocks, pursued by the bloodhounds. We couldn't keep from laughing after we came out of the tent because they were acting on such a small platform that Eliza had to run round and round, and part of the time the one dog they had pursued her, and part of the time she had to pursue the dog. I knew Living would remember, too, so

I took off my waterproof and wrapped it round my books for a baby; then I shouted '*My God! the river!*' just like that—the same as Eliza did in the play; then I leaped from puddle to puddle, and Living and Emma Jane pursued me like the bloodhounds. It's just like that stupid Minnie Smellie who doesn't know a game when she sees one. And Eliza wasn't swearing when she said, 'My God! the river!' It was more like praying."

"Well, you've got no call to be prayin', any more than swearin', in the middle of the road," said Miranda; "but I'm thankful it's no worse. You're born to trouble as the sparks fly upward, an' I'm afraid you allers will be till you learn to bridle your unruly tongue."

"I wish sometimes that I could bridle Minnie's," murmured Rebecca, as she went to set the table for supper.

"I declare she *is* the beatin'est child!" said Miranda, taking off her spectacles and laying down her mending. "You don't think she's a leetle mite crazy, do you, Jane?"

"I don't think she's like the rest of us," responded Jane thoughtfully and with some anxiety in her pleasant face; "but whether it's for the better or the worse I can't hardly tell till she grows up. She's got the making of 'most anything in her, Rebecca has; but I feel sometimes as if we were not fitted to cope with her."

"Stuff an' nonsense!" said Miranda. "Speak for yourself. I feel fitted to cope with any child that ever was born int' the world!"

"I know you do, Mirandy; but that don't *make* you so," returned Jane with a smile.

The habit of speaking her mind freely was certainly growing on Jane to an altogether terrifying extent.

Chapter Ten

Snow-White; Rose-Red

Just before Thanksgiving the affairs of the Simpsons reached what might have been called a crisis, even in their family, which had been born and reared in a state of adventurous poverty and perilous uncertainty.

Riverboro was doing its best to return the entire tribe of Simpsons to the land of its fathers, so to speak, thinking rightly that the town which had given them birth, rather than the town of their adoption, should feed them and keep a roof over their heads until the children were of an age for self-support. There was little to eat in the household and less to wear, though Mrs. Simpson did, as always, her poor best. The children managed to satisfy their appetites by sitting modestly outside their neighbors' kitchen doors when meals were about to be served. They were not exactly popular favorites, but they did receive certain undesirable morsels from the more charitable housewives.

Life was rather dull and dreary, however, and in the chill and gloom of November weather, with the vision of other people's turkeys bursting with fat, and other people's golden pumpkins and squashes and corn being garnered into barns,

the young Simpsons groped about for some inexpensive
form of excitement, and settled upon the selling of soap for
a premium. They had sold enough to their immediate neighbors during the earlier autumn to secure a child's handcart,
which, though very weak on its pins, could be trundled over
the country roads. With large business sagacity and an ex-
ecutive capacity which must have been inherited from their
father, they now proposed to extend their operations to a
larger area and distribute soap to contiguous villages, if
these villages could be induced to buy. The Excelsior Soap
Company paid a very small return of any kind to its infantile
agents, who were scattered through the state, but it in-
flamed their imaginations by the issue of circulars with
highly colored pictures of the premiums to be awarded for
the sale of a certain number of cakes. It was at this juncture
that Clara Belle and Susan Simpson consulted Rebecca, who
threw herself solidly and wholeheartedly into the enterprise, promising her help and that of Emma Jane Perkins.
The premiums within their possible grasp were three: a
bookcase, a plush reclining chair, and a banquet lamp. Of
course the Simpsons had no books, and casting aside, without thought or pang, the plush chair, which might have been
of some use in a family of seven persons (not counting Mr.
Simpson, who ordinarily sat elsewhere at the town's expense), they warmed themselves rapturously in the vision
of the banquet lamp, which speedily became to them more
desirable than food, drink, or clothing. Neither Emma Jane
nor Rebecca perceived anything incongruous in the idea of
the Simpsons striving for a banquet lamp. They looked at
the picture daily and knew that if they themselves were free

agents they would toil, suffer, ay sweat, for the happy privilege of occupying the same room with that lamp through
the coming winter evenings. It looked to be about eight feet
tall in the catalogue, and Emma Jane advised Clara Belle to
measure the height of the Simpson ceilings; but a note in
the margin of the circular informed them that it stood two
and a half feet high when set up in all its dignity and splen-
dor on a proper table, three dollars extra. It was only of polished brass, continued the circular, though it was invariably
mistaken for solid gold, and the shade that accompanied it
(at least it accompanied it if the agent sold a hundred extra
cakes) was of crinkled crêpe paper printed in a dozen delicious hues, from which the joy-dazzled agent might take
his choice.

Seesaw Simpson was not in the syndicate. Clara Belle was
rather a successful agent, but Susan, who could only say
"thoap," never made large returns, and the twins, who were
somewhat young to be thoroughly trustworthy, could be
given only a half dozen cakes at a time, and were obliged to
carry with them on their business trips a brief document
stating the price per cake, dozen, and box. Rebecca and
Emma Jane offered to go two or three miles in some one direction and see what they could do in the way of stirring up
a popular demand for the Snow-White and Rose-Red
brands, the former being devoted to laundry purposes and
the latter being intended for personal use.

There was a great amount of hilarity in the preparation
for this event, and a long council in Emma Jane's attic.
They had the soap company's circular from which to arrange a proper speech, and they had, what was still better,

the remembrance of a certain patent-medicine vender's discourse at the Milltown Fair. His method, when once observed, could never be forgotten; nor his manner, nor his
vocabulary. Emma Jane practiced it on Rebecca, and Rebecca on Emma Jane.

"Can I sell you a little soap this afternoon? It is called
the Snow-White and Rose-Red Soap, six cakes in an ornamental box, only twenty cents for the white, twenty-five
cents for the red. It is made from the purest ingredients, and
if desired could be eaten by an invalid with relish and
profit."

"Oh, Rebecca, don't let's say that!" interposed Emma
Jane hysterically. "It makes me feel like a fool."

"It takes so little to make you feel like a fool, Emma Jane,"
rebuked Rebecca, "that sometimes I think that you must *be*
one. I don't get to feeling like a fool so awfully easy; now
leave out that eating part if you don't like it, and go on."

"The Snow-White is probably the most remarkable laundry soap ever manufactured. Immerse the garments in a
tub, lightly rubbing the more soiled portions with the soap;
leave them submerged in water from sunset to sunrise, and
then the youngest baby can wash them without the slightest
effort."

"*Babe,* not baby," corrected Rebecca from the circular.

"It's just the same thing," argued Emma Jane.

"Of course it's just the same *thing;* but a baby has got to
be called babe or infant in a circular, the same as it is in
poetry! Would you rather say infant?"

"No," grumbled Emma Jane; "infant is worse even than
babe. Rebecca, do you think we'd better do as the circular

says, and let Elijah or Elisha try the soap before we begin
selling?"

"I can't imagine a babe doing a family wash with *any*
soap," answered Rebecca; "but it must be true or they would
never dare to print it, so don't let's bother. Oh! won't it be
the greatest fun, Emma Jane? At some of the houses—where
they can't possibly know me—I shan't be frightened, and I
shall reel off the whole rigmarole, invalid, babe, and all.
Perhaps I shall say even the last sentence, if I can remember
it: 'We sound every chord in the great macro-cosm of satisfaction.'"

This conversation took place on Friday afternoon at
Emma Jane's house, where Rebecca, to her unbounded joy,
was to stay over Sunday, her aunts having gone to Portland
to the funeral of an old friend. Saturday being a holiday,
they were going to have the old white horse, drive to North
Riverboro three miles away, eat a twelve o'clock dinner with
Emma Jane's cousins, and be back at four o'clock punctu-
ally.

When the children asked Mrs. Perkins if they could call at
just a few houses coming and going, and sell a little soap
for the Simpsons, she at first replied decidedly in the nega-
tive. She was an indulgent parent, however, and really had
little objection to Emma Jane amusing herself in this unusual way; it was only for Rebecca, as the niece of the difficult Miranda Sawyer, that she raised scruples; but when
fully persuaded that the enterprise was a charitable one, she
acquiesced.

The girls called at Mr. Watson's store, and arranged for
several large boxes of soap to be charged to Clara Belle

Simpson's account. These were lifted into the back of the wagon, and a happier couple never drove along the country road than Rebecca and her companion. It was a glorious Indian summer day, which suggested nothing of Thanksgiving, near at hand as it was. It was a rustly day, a scarlet and buff, yellow and carmine, bronze and crimson day. There were still many leaves on the oaks and maples, making a goodly show of red and brown and gold. The air was like sparkling cider, and every field had its heaps of yellow and russet good things to eat, all ready for the barns, the mills, and the markets. The horse forgot his twenty years, sniffed the sweet bright air, and trotted like a colt; Nokomis Mountain looked blue and clear in the distance; Rebecca stood in the wagon, and apostrophized the landscape with sudden joy of living:—

> Great, wide, beautiful, wonderful World,
> With the wonderful water round you curled,
> And the wonderful grass upon your breast,
> World, you are beautifully drest!

Dull Emma Jane had never seemed to Rebecca so near, so dear, so tried and true; and Rebecca, to Emma Jane's faithful heart, had never been so brilliant, so bewildering, so fascinating, as in this visit together, with its intimacy, its freedom, and the added delights of an exciting business enterprise.

Chapter Eleven

Mr. Aladdin

A single hour's experience of the vicissitudes incident to a business career clouded the children's spirits just the least bit. They did not accompany each other to the doors of their chosen victims, feeling sure that together they could not approach the subject seriously; but they parted at the gate of each house, the one holding the horse while the other took the soap samples and interviewed anyone who seemed of a coming-on disposition. Emma Jane had disposed of three single cakes, Rebecca of three small boxes; for a difference in their ability to persuade the public was clearly defined at the start, though neither of them ascribed either success or defeat to anything but the imperious force of circumstances. Housewives looked at Emma Jane and desired no soap; listened to her description of its merits, and still desired none. Other stars in their courses governed Rebecca's doings. The people whom she interviewed either remembered their present need of soap, or reminded themselves that they would need it in the future; the notable point in the case being that lucky Rebecca accomplished, with almost no effort, results that poor little Emma Jane failed to attain by hard and conscientious labor.

"It's your turn, Rebecca, and I'm glad, too," said Emma Jane, drawing up to a gateway and indicating a house that was set a considerable distance from the road. "I haven't got over trembling from the last place yet." (A lady had put her head out of an upstairs window and called, "Go away, little girl; whatever you have in your box we don't want any.") "I don't know who lives here, and the blinds are all shut in front. If there's nobody at home you mustn't count it, but take the next house as yours."

Rebecca walked up the lane and went to the side door. There was a porch there, and seated in a rocking-chair, husking corn, was a good-looking young man, or was he middle-aged? Rebecca could not make up her mind. At all events he had an air of the city about him,—well-shaven face, well-trimmed mustache, well-fitting clothes. Rebecca was a trifle shy at this unexpected encounter, but there was nothing to be done but explain her presence, so she asked, "Is the lady of the house at home?"

"I am the lady of the house at present," said the stranger, with a whimsical smile. "What can I do for you?"

"Have you ever heard of the—would you like, or I mean—do you need any soap?" queried Rebecca.

"Do I look as if I did?" he responded unexpectedly.

Rebecca dimpled. "I didn't mean *that;* I have some soap to sell; I mean I would like to introduce to you a very re-markable soap, the best now on the market. It is called the—"

"Oh! I must know that soap," said the gentleman genially. "Made out of pure vegetable fats, isn't it?"

"The very purest," corroborated Rebecca.

"No acid in it?"

"Not a trace."

"And yet a child could do the Monday washing with it and use no force."

"A babe," corrected Rebecca.

"Oh! a babe, eh? That child grows younger every year, instead of older—wise child!"

This was great good fortune, to find a customer who knew all the virtues of the article in advance. Rebecca dimpled more and more, and at her new friend's invitation sat down on a stool at his side near the edge of the porch. The beauties of the ornamental box which held the Red-Rose were disclosed, and the prices of both that and the Snow-White were unfolded. Presently she forgot all about her silent partner at the gate and was talking as if she had known this grand personage all her life.

"I'm keeping house to-day, but I don't live here," explained the delightful gentleman. "I'm just on a visit to my aunt, who has gone to Portland. I used to be here as a boy, and I am very fond of the spot."

"I don't think anything takes the place of the farm where one lived when one was a child," observed Rebecca, nearly bursting with pride at having at last successfully used the indefinite pronoun in general conversation.

The man darted a look at her and put down his ear of corn. "So you consider your childhood a thing of the past, do you, young lady?"

"I can still remember it," answered Rebecca gravely, "though it seems a long time ago."

"I can remember mine well enough, and a particularly unpleasant one it was," said the stranger.

"So was mine," sighed Rebecca. "What was your worst trouble?"

"Lack of food and clothes principally."

"Oh!" exclaimed Rebecca sympathetically—"mine was no shoes and too many babies and not enough books. But you're all right and happy now, aren't you?" she asked doubtfully, for though he looked handsome, well-fed, and prosperous, any child could see that his eyes were tired and his mouth was sad when he was not speaking.

"I'm doing pretty well, thank you," said the man, with a delightful smile. "Now tell me, how much soap ought I to buy to-day?"

"How much has your aunt on hand now?" suggested the very modest and inexperienced agent; "and how much would she need?"

"Oh, I don't know about that; soap keeps, doesn't it?"

"I'm not certain," said Rebecca conscientiously, "but I'll look in the circular—it's sure to tell"; and she drew the document from her pocket.

"What are you going to do with the magnificent profits you get from this business?"

"We are not selling for our own benefit," said Rebecca confidentially. "My friend who is holding the horse at the gate is the daughter of a very rich blacksmith, and doesn't need any money. I am poor, but I live with my aunts in a brick house, and of course they wouldn't like me to be a ped-dler. We are trying to get a premium for some friends of ours."

Rebecca had never thought of alluding to the circum-stances with her previous customers, but unexpectedly she found herself describing Mr. Simpson, Mrs. Simpson, and the Simpson family; their poverty, their joyless life, and their abject need of a banquet lamp to brighten their exist-ence.

"You needn't argue that point," laughed the man, as he stood up to get a glimpse of the "rich blacksmith's daugh-ter" at the gate. "I can see that they ought to have it if they want it, and especially if you want them to have it. I've known what it was myself to do without a banquet lamp. Now give me the circular, and let's do some figuring. How much do the Simpsons lack at this moment?"

"If they sell two hundred more cakes this month and next, they can have the lamp by Christmas," Rebecca an-swered, "and they can get a shade by summer time; but I'm afraid I can't help very much after to-day, because my Aunt Miranda may not like to have me."

"I see. Well, that's all right. I'll take three hundred cakes, and that will give them shade and all."

Rebecca had been seated on a stool very near to the edge of the porch, and at this remark she made a sudden move-ment, tipped over, and disappeared into a clump of lilac bushes. It was a very short distance, fortunately, and the amused capitalist picked her up, set her on her feet, and brushed her off. "You should never seem surprised when

you have taken a large order," said he; "you ought to have replied, 'Can't you make it three hundred and fifty?' instead of capsizing in that unbusinesslike way."

"Oh, I could never say anything like that!" exclaimed Rebecca, who was blushing crimson at her awkward fall. "But it doesn't seem right for you to buy so much. Are you sure you can afford it?"

"If I can't, I'll save on something else," returned the jocose philanthropist.

"What if your aunt shouldn't like the kind of soap?" queried Rebecca nervously.

"My aunt always likes what I like," he returned.

"Mine doesn't!" exclaimed Rebecca.

"Then there's something wrong with your aunt!"

"Or with me," laughed Rebecca.

"What is your name, young lady?"

"Rebecca Rowena Randall, sir."

"What?" with an amused smile. "*Both?* Your mother was generous."

"She couldn't bear to give up either of the names, she says."

"Do you want to hear my name?"

"I think I know already," answered Rebecca, with a bright glance. "I'm sure you must be Mr. Aladdin in the 'Arabian Nights.' Oh, please, can I run down and tell Emma Jane? She must be so tired waiting, and she will be so glad!"

At the man's nod of assent Rebecca sped down the lane, crying irrepressibly as she neared the wagon, "Oh, Emma Jane! Emma Jane! we are sold out!"

Mr. Aladdin followed smilingly to corroborate this astonishing, unbelievable statement; lifted all their boxes from the back of the wagon, and taking the circular, promised to write to the Excelsior Company that night concerning the premium.

"If you could contrive to keep a secret, you two little girls, it would be rather a nice surprise to have the lamp arrive at the Simpsons' on Thanksgiving Day, wouldn't it?" he asked, as he tucked the old lap-robe cozily over their feet.

They gladly assented, and broke into a chorus of excited thanks, during which tears of joy stood in Rebecca's eyes.

"Oh, don't mention it!" laughed Mr. Aladdin, lifting his hat. "I was a sort of commercial traveler myself once,— years ago,—and I like to see the thing well done. Good-bye, Miss Rebecca Rowena! Just let me know whenever you have anything to sell, for I'm certain beforehand I shall want it."

"Good-bye, Mr. Aladdin! I surely will!" cried Rebecca, tossing back her dark braids delightedly and waving her hand.

"Oh, Rebecca!" said Emma Jane in an awe-struck whisper. "He raised his hat to us, and we not thirteen! It'll be five years before we're ladies."

"Never mind," answered Rebecca, "we are the *beginnings* of ladies, even now."

"He tucked the lap-robe round us, too," continued Emma Jane, in an ecstasy of reminiscence. "Oh! isn't he perfectly elegant? And wasn't it lovely of him to buy us out? And just think of having both the lamp and the shade for one

day's work! Aren't you glad you wore your pink gingham
now, even if Mother did make you put on flannel underneath? You do look so pretty in pink and red, Rebecca, and
so homely in drab and brown!"

"I know it," sighed Rebecca. "I wish I was like you—
pretty in all colors!" And Rebecca looked longingly at
Emma Jane's fat, rosy cheeks; at her blue eyes, which said
nothing; at her neat nose, which had no character; at her
red lips, from between which no word worth listening to had
ever issued.

"Never mind!" said Emma Jane comfortingly. "Everybody says you're awful bright and smart, and Mother thinks
you'll be better looking all the time as you grow older. You
wouldn't believe it, but I was a dreadful homely baby, and
homely right along till a year or two ago, when my red hair
began to grow dark. What was the nice man's name?"

"I never thought to ask!" ejaculated Rebecca. "Aunt Miranda would say that was just like me, and it is. But I called
him Mr. Aladdin because he gave us a lamp. You know the
story of Aladdin and the wonderful lamp?"

"Oh, Rebecca! how could you call him a nickname the
very first time you ever saw him?"

"Aladdin isn't a nickname exactly; anyway, he laughed
and seemed to like it."

By dint of superhuman effort, and putting such a seal
upon their lips as never mortals put before, the two girls
succeeded in keeping their wonderful news to themselves;
although it was obvious to all beholders that they were in an
extraordinary and abnormal state of mind.

On Thanksgiving the lamp arrived in a large packing-box, and was taken out and set up by Seesaw Simpson, who suddenly began to admire and respect the business ability of his sisters. Rebecca had heard the news of its arrival, but waited until nearly dark before asking permission to go to the Simpsons', so that she might see the gorgeous trophy lighted and sending a blaze of crimson glory through its red crêpe paper shade.

Chapter Twelve

The Banquet Lamp

There had been company at the brick house to the bountiful Thanksgiving dinner which had been provided at one o'clock,—the Burnham sisters, who lived between North Riverboro and Shaker Village, and who for more than a quarter of a century had come to pass the holiday with the Sawyers every year.

Rebecca sat silent with a book after the dinner dishes were washed, and when it was nearly five asked if she might go to the Simpsons'.

"What do you want to run after those Simpson children for on a Thanksgiving Day?" queried Miss Miranda. "Can't you set still for once and listen to the improvin' conversation of your elders? You never can let well enough alone, but want to be forever on the move."

"The Simpsons have a new lamp, and Emma Jane and I promised to go up and see it lighted, and make it a kind of a party."

"What under the canopy did they want of a lamp, and where did they get the money to pay for it? If Abner was at home, I should think he'd been swappin' again," said Miss Miranda.

"The children got it as a prize for selling soap," replied Rebecca; "they've been working for a year, and you know I told you that Emma Jane and I helped them the Saturday afternoon you were in Portland."

"I didn't take notice, I s'pose, for it's the first time I ever heard the lamp mentioned. Well, you can go for an hour, and no more. Remember it's as dark at six as it is at midnight. Would you like to take along some Baldwin apples? What have you got in the pocket of that new dress that makes it sag down so?"

"It's my nuts and raisins from dinner," replied Rebecca, who never succeeded in keeping the most innocent action a secret from her Aunt Miranda; "they're just what you gave me on my plate."

"Why didn't you eat them?"

"Because I'd had enough dinner, and I thought if I saved these, it would make the Simpsons' party better," stammered Rebecca, who hated to be scolded and examined before company.

"They were your own, Rebecca," interposed Aunt Jane, "and if you chose to save them to give away, it is all right. We ought never to let this day pass without giving our neighbors something to be thankful for, instead of taking all the time to think of our own mercies."

The Burnham sisters nodded approvingly as Rebecca went out, and remarked that they had never seen a child grow and improve so fast in so short a time.

"There's plenty of room left for more improvement, as

you'd know if she lived in the same house with you," answered Miranda. "She's into every namable thing in the neighborhood, an' not only into it, but generally at the head an' front of it, especially when it's mischief. Of all the foolishness I ever heard of, that lamp beats everything; it's just like those Simpsons, but I didn't suppose the children had brains enough to sell anything."

"One of them must have," said Miss Ellen Burnham, "for the girl that was selling soap at the Ladds' in North Riverboro was described by Adam Ladd as the most remarkable and winning child he ever saw."

"It must have been Clara Belle, and I should never call her remarkable," answered Miss Miranda. "Has Adam been home again?"

"Yes, he's been staying a few days with his aunt. There's no limit to the money he's making, they say; and he always brings presents for all the neighbors. This time it was a full set of furs for Mrs. Ladd; and to think we can remember the time he was a barefoot boy without two shirts to his back! It is strange he hasn't married, with all his money, and him so fond of children that he always has a pack of them at his heels."

"There's hope for him still, though," said Miss Jane smilingly; "for I don't s'pose he's more than thirty."

"He could get a wife in Riverboro if he was a hundred and thirty," remarked Miss Miranda.

"Adam's aunt says he was so taken with the little girl that sold the soap (Clara Belle, did you say her name was?), that he declared he was going to bring her a Christmas present," continued Miss Ellen.

"Well, there's no accountin' for tastes," exclaimed Miss Miranda. "Clara Belle's got cross-eyes and red hair, but I'd be the last one to grudge her a Christmas present; the more Adam Ladd gives to her the less the town'll have to."

"Isn't there another Simpson girl?" asked Miss Lydia Burnham; "for this one couldn't have been cross-eyed; I remember Mrs. Ladd saying Adam remarked about this child's handsome eyes. He said it was her eyes that made him buy the three hundred cakes. Mrs. Ladd has it stacked up in the shed chamber."

"Three hundred cakes!" ejaculated Miranda. "Well, there's one crop that never fails in Riverboro!"

"What's that?" asked Miss Lydia politely.

"The fool crop," responded Miranda tersely, and changed the subject, much to Jane's gratitude, for she had been nervous and ill at ease for the last fifteen minutes. What child in Riverboro could be described as remarkable and winning, save Rebecca? What child had wonderful eyes, except the same Rebecca? And finally, was there ever a child in the world who could make a man buy soap by the hundred cakes, save Rebecca?

Meantime the "remarkable" child had flown up the road in the deepening dusk, but she had not gone far before she heard the sound of hurrying footsteps, and saw a well-known figure coming in her direction. In a moment she and Emma Jane met and exchanged a breathless embrace.

"Something awful has happened," panted Emma Jane.

"Don't tell me it's broken," exclaimed Rebecca.

"No! oh, no! not that! It was packed in straw, and every piece came out all right; and I was there, and I never said a single thing about your selling the three hundred cakes that got the lamp, so that we could be together when you told."

"*Our* selling the three hundred cakes," corrected Rebecca; "you did as much as I."

"No, I didn't, Rebecca Randall. I just sat at the gate and held the horse."

"Yes, but *whose* horse was it that took us to North Riverboro? And besides, it just happened to be my turn. If you had gone in and found Mr. Aladdin you would have had the wonderful lamp given to you; but what's the trouble?"

"The Simpsons have no kerosene and no wicks. I guess they thought a banquet lamp was something that lighted itself, and burned without any help. Seesaw has gone to the doctor's to try if he can borrow a wick, and mother let me have a pint of oil, but she says she won't give me any more, We never thought of the expense of keeping up the lamp, Rebecca."

"No, we didn't, but let's not worry about that till after the party. I have a handful of nuts and raisins and some apples."

"I have peppermints and maple sugar," said Emma Jane. "They had a real Thanksgiving dinner; the doctor gave them sweet potatoes and cranberries and turnips; father sent a sparerib, and Mrs. Cobb a chicken and a jar of mincemeat."

At half-past five one might have looked in at the Simpsons' windows, and seen the party at its height. Mrs. Simpson had let the kitchen fire die out, and had brought the baby to grace the festal scene. The lamp seemed to be having the party, and receiving the guests. The children had

taken the one small table in the house, and it was placed in
the far corner of the room to serve as a pedestal. On it stood
the sacred, the adored, the long-desired object; almost as
beautiful, and nearly half as large as the advertisement.
The brass glistened like gold, and the crimson paper shade
glowed like a giant ruby. In the wide splash of light that it
flung upon the floor sat the Simpsons, in reverent and sol-
emn silence, Emma Jane standing behind them, hand in
hand with Rebecca. There seemed to be no desire for conversation; the occasion was too thrilling and serious for that.
The lamp, it was tacitly felt by everybody, was dignifying
the party, and providing sufficient entertainment simply by
its presence; being fully as satisfactory in its way as a pian-
ola or a string band.

"I wish father could see it," said Clara Belle loyally.

"If he onth thaw it he'd want to thwap it," murmured
Susan sagaciously.

At the appointed hour Rebecca dragged herself reluctantly away from the enchanting scene.

"I'll turn the lamp out the minute I think you and Emma
Jane are home," said Clara Belle. "And, oh! I'm so glad you
both live where you can see it shine from our windows. I
wonder how long it will burn without bein' filled if I only
keep it lit one hour every night?"

"You needn't put it out for want o' karosene," said Seesaw,
coming in from the shed, "for there's a great kag of it settin'
out there. Mr. Tubbs brought it over from North Riverboro
and said somebody sent an order by mail for it."

Rebecca squeezed Emma Jane's arm, and Emma Jane
gave a rapturous return squeeze. "It was Mr. Aladdin,"

whispered Rebecca, as they ran down the path to the gate. Seesaw followed them and handsomely offered to see them "a piece" down the road, but Rebecca declined his escort with such decision that he did not press the matter, but went to bed to dream of her instead. In his dreams flashes of lightning proceeded from both her eyes, and she held a flaming sword in either hand.

Rebecca entered the home dining-room joyously. The Burnham sisters had gone and the two aunts were knitting.

"It was a heavenly party," she cried, taking off her hat and cape.

"Go back and see if you have shut the door tight, and then lock it," said Miss Miranda, in her usual austere manner.

"It was a heavenly party," reiterated Rebecca, coming in again, much too excited to be easily crushed, "and oh! Aunt Jane, Aunt Miranda, if you'll only come into the kitchen and look out of the sink window, you can see the banquet lamp shining all red, just as if the Simpsons' house was on fire."

"And probably it will be before long," observed Miranda. "I've got no patience with such foolish goin's-on."

Jane accompanied Rebecca into the kitchen. Although the feeble glimmer which she was able to see from that distance did not seem to her a dazzling exhibition, she tried to be as enthusiastic as possible.

"Rebecca, who was it that sold the three hundred cakes of soap to Mr. Ladd in North Riverboro?"

"Mr. *Who?*" exclaimed Rebecca.

"Mr. Ladd, in North Riverboro."

"Is that his real name?" queried Rebecca in astonishment. "I didn't make a bad guess." And she laughed softly to herself.

"I asked you who sold the soap to Adam Ladd?" resumed Miss Jane.

"Adam Ladd! Then he's A. Ladd, too; what fun!"

"Answer me, Rebecca."

"Oh! excuse me, Aunt Jane, I was so busy thinking. Emma Jane and I sold the soap to Mr. Ladd."

"Did you tease him, or make him buy it?"

"Now, Aunt Jane, how could I make a big grown-up man buy anything if he didn't want to? He needed the soap dreadfully as a present for his aunt."

Miss Jane still looked a little unconvinced, though she only said, "I hope your Aunt Miranda won't mind, but you know how particular she is, Rebecca, and I really wish you wouldn't do anything out of the ordinary without asking her first, for your actions are very queer."

"There can't be anything wrong this time," Rebecca answered confidently. "Emma Jane sold her cakes to her own relations and to Uncle Jerry Cobb, and I went first to those new tenements near the lumber mill, and then to the Ladds'. Mr. Ladd bought all we had and made us promise to keep the secret until the premium came, and I've been going about ever since as if the banquet lamp was inside of me all lighted up and burning, for everybody to see."

Rebecca's hair was loosened and falling over her forehead in ruffled waves; her eyes were brilliant, her cheeks crimson; there was a hint of everything in the girl's face,—of sensitiveness and delicacy as well as of ardor; there was the sweetness of the mayflower and the strength of the young oak, but one could easily divine that she was one of

> The souls by nature pitched too high,
> By suffering plunged too low.

"That's just the way you look, for all the world as if you did have a lamp burning inside of you," sighed Aunt Jane. "Rebecca! Rebecca! I wish you could take things easier, child; I am fearful for you sometimes."

Chapter Thirteen

Seasons of Growth

The days flew by; as summer had melted into autumn so autumn had given place to winter. Life in the brick house had gone on more placidly of late, for Rebecca was honestly trying to be more careful in the performance of her tasks and duties as well as more quiet in her play, and she was slowly learning the power of the soft answer in turning away wrath.

Miranda had not had, perhaps, quite as many opportunities in which to lose her temper, but it is only just to say that she had not fully availed herself of all that had offered themselves.

There had been one outburst of righteous wrath occasioned by Rebecca's over-hospitable habits, which were later shown in a still more dramatic and unexpected fashion.

On a certain Friday afternoon she asked her Aunt Miranda if she might take half her bread and milk upstairs to a friend.

"What friend have you got up there, for pity's sake?" demanded Aunt Miranda.

"The Simpson baby, come to stay over Sunday; that is, if you're willing, Mrs. Simpson says she is. Shall I bring her down and show her? She's dressed in an old dress of Emma Jane's and she looks sweet."

"You can bring her down, but you can't show her to me! You can smuggle her out the way you smuggled her in and take her back to her mother. Where on earth do you get your notions, borrowing a baby for Sunday!"

"You're so used to a house without a baby you don't know how dull it is," sighed Rebecca resignedly, as she moved towards the door; "but at the farm there was always a nice fresh one to play with and cuddle. There were too many, but that's not half as bad as none at all. Well, I'll take her back. She'll be dreadfully disappointed and so will Mrs. Simpson. She was planning to go to Milltown."

"She can un-plan then," observed Miss Miranda.

"Perhaps I can go up there and take care of the baby?" suggested Rebecca. "I brought her home so 't I could do my Saturday work just the same."

"You've got enough to do right here, without any borrowed babies to make more steps. Now, no answering back, just give the child some supper and carry it home where it belongs."

"You don't want me to go down the front way. Hadn't I better just come through this room and let you look at her? She has yellow hair and big blue eyes! Mrs. Simpson says she takes after her father."

Miss Miranda smiled acidly as she said she couldn't take after her father, for he'd take anything there was before she got there!

Aunt Jane was in the linen closet upstairs, sorting out the clean sheets and pillow cases for Saturday, and Rebecca sought comfort from her.

"I brought the Simpson baby home, Aunt Jane, thinking it would help us over a dull Sunday, but Aunt Miranda won't let her stay. Emma Jane has the promise of her next Sunday and Alice Robinson the next. Mrs. Simpson wanted I should have her first because I've had so much experience in babies. Come in and look at her sitting up in my bed, Aunt Jane! Isn't she lovely? She's the fat, gurgly kind, not thin and fussy like some babies, and I thought I was going to have her to undress and dress twice each day. Oh dear! I wish I could have a printed book with everything set down in it that I *could* do, and then I wouldn't get disappointed so often."

"No book could be printed that would fit you, Rebecca," answered Aunt Jane, "for nobody could imagine beforehand the things you'd want to do. Are you going to carry that heavy child home in your arms?"

"No, I'm going to drag her in the little soapwagon. Come, baby! Take your thumb out of your mouth and come to ride with Becky in your go-cart." She stretched out her strong young arms to the crowing baby, sat down in a chair with the child, turned her upside down unceremoniously, took from her waistband and scornfully flung away a crooked pin, walked with her (still in a highly reversed position) to the bureau, selected a large safety pin, and proceeded to attach her brief red flannel petticoat to a sort of shirt that she wore. Whether flat on her stomach, or head down, heels in the air, the Simpson baby knew she was in the hands of an expert, and continued gurgling placidly while Aunt Jane regarded the pantomime with a kind of dazed awe.

"Bless my soul, Rebecca," she ejaculated, "it beats all how handy you are with babies!"

"I ought to be; I've brought up three and a half of 'em," Rebecca responded cheerfully, pulling up the infant Simpson's stockings.

"I should think you'd be fonder of dolls than you are," said Jane.

"I do like them, but there's never any change in a doll; it's always the same everlasting old doll, and you have to make believe it's cross or sick, or it loves you, or can't bear you. Babies are more trouble, but nicer."

Miss Jane stretched out a thin hand with a slender, worn band of gold on the finger, and the baby curled her dimpled fingers round it and held it fast.

"You wear a ring on your engagement finger, don't you, Aunt Jane? Did you ever think about getting married?"

"Yes, dear, long ago."

"What happened, Aunt Jane?"

"He died—just before."

"Oh!" And Rebecca's eyes grew misty.

"He was a soldier and he died of a gunshot wound, in a hospital, down South."

"Oh! Aunt Jane!" softly. "Away from you?"

"No, I was with him."

"Was he young?"

"Yes; young and brave and handsome, Rebecca; he was Mr. Carter's brother Tom."

"Oh! I'm so glad you were with him! Wasn't he glad, Aunt Jane?"

Jane looked back across the half-forgotten years, and the vision of Tom's gladness flashed upon her: his haggard smile, the tears in his tired eyes, his outstretched arms, his weak voice saying, "Oh, Jenny! Dear Jenny! I've wanted you so, Jenny!" It was too much! She had never breathed a word of it before to a human creature, for there was no one who would have understood. Now, in a shamefaced way, to hide her brimming eyes, she put her head down on the young shoulder beside her, saying, "It was hard, Rebecca!"

The Simpson baby had cuddled down sleeping in Rebecca's lap, leaning her head back and sucking her thumb contentedly. Rebecca put her cheek down until it touched her aunt's gray hair and softly patted her, as she said, "I'm sorry, Aunt Jane!"

The girl's eyes were soft and tender and the heart within her stretched a little and grew; grew in sweetness and intuition and depth of feeling. It had looked into another heart, felt it beat, and heard it sigh; and that is how all hearts grow.

Episodes like these enlivened the quiet course of everyday existence, made more quiet by the departure of Dick Carter, Living Perkins, and Huldah Meserve for Wareham, and the small attendance at the winter school, from which the younger children of the place stayed away during the cold weather.

Life, however, could never be thoroughly dull or lacking in adventure to a child of Rebecca's temperament. Her nature was full of adaptability, fluidity, receptivity. She made

friends everywhere she went, and snatched up acquaintances in every corner.

It was she who ran to the shed door to take the dish to the "meat man" or "fish man"; she who knew the family histories of the itinerant fruit venders and tin peddlers; she who was asked to take supper or pass the night with children in neighboring villages—children of whose parents her aunts had never so much as heard. As to the nature of these friendships, which seemed so many to the eye of the superficial observer, they were of various kinds, and while the girl pursued them with enthusiasm and ardor, they left her unsatisfied and heart-hungry; they were never intimacies such as are so readily made by shallow natures. She loved Emma Jane, but it was a friendship born of propinquity and circumstance, not of true affinity. It was her neighbor's amiability, constancy, and devotion that she loved, and although she rated these qualities at their true value, she was always searching beyond them for intellectual treasures; searching and never finding, for although Emma Jane had the advantage in years she was still immature. Huldah Meserve had an instinctive love of fun which appealed to Rebecca; she also had a fascinating knowledge of the world, from having visited her married sisters in Milltown and Portland; but on the other hand there was a certain sharpness and lack of sympathy in Huldah which repelled rather than attracted. With Dick Carter she could at least talk intelligently about lessons. He was a very ambitious boy, full of plans for his future, which he discussed quite freely with Rebecca, but when she broached the subject of her future his interest sensibly lessened. Into the world of the ideal Emma Jane, Huldah, and Dick alike never seemed to have peeped, and the consciousness of this was always a fixed gulf between them and Rebecca.

"Uncle Jerry" and "Aunt Sarah" Cobb were dear friends of quite another sort, a very satisfying and perhaps a somewhat dangerous one. A visit from Rebecca always sent them into a twitter of delight. Her merry conversation and quaint comments on life in general fairly dazzled the old couple, who hung on her lightest word as if it had been a prophet's utterance; and Rebecca, though she had had no previous experience, owned to herself a perilous pleasure in being dazzling, even to a couple of dear humdrum old people like Mr. and Mrs. Cobb. Aunt Sarah flew to the pantry and cellar whenever Rebecca's slim little shape first appeared on the crest of the hill, and a jelly tart or a frosted cake was sure to be forthcoming. The sight of old Uncle Jerry's spare figure in its clean white shirt sleeves, whatever the weather, always made Rebecca's heart warm when she saw him peer longingly from the kitchen window. Before the snow came, many was the time he had come out to sit on a pile of boards at the gate, to see if by any chance she was mounting the hill that led to their house. In the autumn Rebecca was often the old man's companion while he was digging potatoes or shelling beans, and now in the winter, when a younger man was driving the stage, she sometimes stayed with him while he did his evening milking. It is safe to say that he was the only creature in Riverboro who possessed Rebecca's entire confidence; the only being to whom she poured out her whole heart, with its wealth of hopes, and dreams, and vague ambitions. At the brick house she practiced scales and exercises, but at the Cobbs' cabinet organ she sang like a bird, improvising simple accompaniments that seemed to her ignorant auditors nothing short of marvelous. Here she was happy, here she was loved, here she was drawn out of herself and admired and made much of. But, she thought, if there were somebody who not only loved but understood; who spoke her language, comprehended her desires, and responded to her mysterious longings! Perhaps in the big world of Wareham there would be people who thought and dreamed and wondered as she did.

In reality Jane did not understand her niece very much better than Miranda; the difference between the sisters was, that while Jane was puzzled, she was also attracted, and when she was quite in the dark for an explanation of some quaint or unusual action she was sympathetic as to its possible motive and believed the best. A greater change had come over Jane than over any other person in the brick house, but it had been wrought so secretly, and concealed so religiously, that it scarcely appeared to the ordinary observer. Life had now a motive utterly lacking before. Breakfast was not eaten in the kitchen, because it seemed worth while, now that there were three persons, to lay the cloth in the dining-room; it was also a more bountiful meal than of yore, when there was no child to consider. The morning was made cheerful by Rebecca's start for school, the packing of the luncheon basket, the final word about umbrella, waterproof, or rubbers; the parting admonition and the unconscious waiting at the window for the last wave of the hand. She found herself taking pride in Rebecca's improved appearance, her rounded throat and cheeks, and her better color; she was wont to mention the length of Rebecca's hair and add a word as to its remarkable evenness and luster, at times when Mrs. Perkins grew too diffuse about Emma Jane's complexion. She threw herself wholeheartedly on her niece's side when it became a question between a crimson or a brown linsey-woolsey dress, and went through a memorable struggle with her sister concerning the purchase of a red bird for Rebecca's black felt hat. No one guessed the quiet pleasure that lay hidden in her heart when she watched the girl's dark head bent over her lessons at night, nor dreamed of her joy in certain quiet evenings when Miranda went to prayer meeting; evenings when Rebecca would read aloud "Hiawatha" or "Barbara Frietchie," "The Bugle Song," or "The Brook." Her narrow, humdrum existence bloomed under the dews that fell from this fresh spirit; her dullness brightened under the kindling touch of the younger mind, took fire from the "vital spark of heavenly flame" that seemed always to radiate from Rebecca's presence.

Rebecca's idea of being a painter, like her friend Miss Ross, was gradually receding, owing to the apparently insuperable difficulties in securing any instruction. Her Aunt Miranda saw no wisdom in cultivating such a talent, and could not conceive that any money could ever be earned by its exercise. "Hand-painted pictures" were held in little esteem in Riverboro, where the cheerful chromo or the dignified steel engraving were respected and valued. There was a slight, a very slight hope, that Rebecca might be allowed a few music lessons from Miss Morton, who played the church cabinet organ, but this depended entirely upon

whether Mrs. Morton would decide to accept a hayrack in
return for a year's instruction from her daughter. She had
the matter under advisement, but a doubt as to whether or
not she would sell or rent her hayfields kept her from coming
to a conclusion. Music, in common with all other accomp-
lishments, was viewed by Miss Miranda as a trivial, useless, and foolish amusement, but she allowed Rebecca an
hour a day for practice on the old piano, and a little extra
time for lessons, if Jane could secure them without payment
of actual cash.

The news from Sunnybrook Farm was hopeful rather than
otherwise. Cousin Ann's husband had died, and John, Rebecca's favorite brother, had gone to be the man of the
house to the widowed cousin. He was to have good schooling in return for his care of the horse and cow and barn,
and what was still more dazzling, the use of the old doctor's medical library of two or three dozen volumes. John's
whole heart was set on becoming a country doctor, with
Rebecca to keep house for him, and the vision seemed now
so true, so near, that he could almost imagine his horse
ploughing through snowdrifts on errands of mercy, or, less
dramatic but none the less attractive, could see a physician's
neat turnout trundling along the shady country roads, a
medicine case between his, Dr. Randall's, feet, and Miss Rebecca Randall sitting in a black silk dress by his side.

Hannah now wore her hair in a coil and her dresses a
trifle below her ankles, these concessions being due to her
extreme height. Mark had broken his collar bone, but it was
healing well. Little Mira was growing very pretty. There
was even a rumor that the projected railroad from Temper-

ance to Plumville might go near the Randall farm, in which case land would rise in value from nothing-at-all an acre to something at least resembling a price. Mrs. Randall refused to consider any improvement in their financial condition as a possibility. Content to work from sunrise to sunset to gain a mere subsistence for her children, she lived in their future, not in her own present, as a mother is wont to do when her own lot seems hard and cheerless.

Chapter Fourteen

Gray Days and Gold

When Rebecca looked back upon the year or two that followed the Simpsons' Thanksgiving party, she could see only certain milestones rising in the quiet pathway of the months.

The first milestone was Christmas Day. It was a fresh, crystal morning, with icicles hanging like dazzling pendants from the trees and a glaze of pale blue on the surface of the snow. The Simpsons' red barn stood out, a glowing mass of color in the white landscape. Rebecca had been busy for weeks before, trying to make a present for each of the seven persons at Sunnybrook Farm, a somewhat difficult proceeding on an expenditure of fifty cents, hoarded by incredible exertion. Success had been achieved, however, and the precious packet had been sent by post two days previous. Miss Sawyer had bought her niece a nice gray squirrel muff and tippet, which was even more unbecoming, if possible, than Rebecca's other articles of wearing apparel; but Aunt Jane had made her the loveliest dress of green cashmere, a soft, soft green like that of a young leaf. It was very simply made, but the color delighted the eye. Then there was a beautiful "tatting" collar from her mother, some scarlet mittens from Mrs. Cobb, and a handkerchief from Emma Jane.

Rebecca herself had fashioned an elaborate tea-cozy with a letter "M" in outline stitch, and a pretty frilled pincushion marked with a "J," for her two aunts, so that taken all together the day would have been an unequivocal success had nothing else happened; but something else did.

There was a knock at the door at breakfast time, and Rebecca, answering it, was asked by a boy if Miss Rebecca Randall lived there. On being told that she did, he handed her a parcel bearing her name, a parcel which she took like one in a dream and bore into the dining-room.

"It's a present; it must be," she said, looking at it in a dazed sort of way; "but I can't think who it could be from."

"A good way to find out would be to open it," remarked Miss Miranda.

The parcel being untied proved to have two smaller packages within, and Rebecca opened with trembling fingers the one addressed to her. Anybody's fingers would have trembled. There was a case which, when the cover was lifted, disclosed a long chain of delicate pink coral beads,— a chain ending in a cross made of coral rosebuds. A card with "Merry Christmas from Mr. Aladdin" lay under the cross.

"Of all things!" exclaimed the two old ladies, rising in their seats. "Who sent it?"

"Mr. Ladd," said Rebecca under her breath.

"Adam Ladd! Well, I never! Don't you remember Ellen

Burnham said he was going to send Rebecca a Christmas present? But I never supposed he'd think of it again," said Jane. "What's the other package?"

It proved to be a silver chain with a blue enamel locket on it, marked for Emma Jane. That added the last touch—to have him remember them both! There was a letter also, which ran:—

DEAR MISS REBECCA ROWENA,—My idea of a Christmas present is' something entirely unnecessary and useless. I have always noticed when I give this sort of thing that people love it, so I hope I have not chosen wrong for you and your friend. You must wear your chain this afternoon, please, and let me see it on your neck, for I am coming over in my new sleigh to take you both to drive. My aunt is delighted with the soap.

Sincerely your friend,

ADAM LADD.

"Well, well!" cried Miss Jane, "isn't that kind of him? He's very fond of children, Lyddy Burnham says. Now eat your breakfast, Rebecca, and after we've done the dishes you can run over to Emma's and give her her chain— What's the matter, child?"

Rebecca's emotions seemed always to be stored, as it were, in adjoining compartments, and to be continually getting mixed. At this moment, though her joy was too deep for words, her bread-and-butter almost choked her, and at intervals a tear stole furtively down her cheek.

Mr. Ladd called as he promised, and made the acquaintance of the aunts, understanding them both in five minutes as well as if he had known them for years. On a footstool near the open fire sat Rebecca, silent and shy, so conscious of her fine apparel and the presence of Aunt Miranda that she could not utter a word. It was one of her "beauty days." Happiness, excitement, the color of the green dress, and the touch of lovely pink in the coral necklace had transformed the little brown wren for the time into a bird of plumage, and Adam Ladd watched her with evident satisfaction. Then there was the sleigh ride, during which she found her tongue and chattered like any magpie, and so ended that glorious Christmas Day; and many and many a night thereafter did Rebecca go to sleep with the precious coral chain under her pillow, one hand always upon it to be certain that it was safe.

Another milestone was the departure of the Simpsons from Riverboro, bag and baggage, the banquet lamp being their most conspicuous possession. It was delightful to be rid of Seesaw's hateful presence; but otherwise the loss of several playmates at one fell swoop made rather a gap in Riverboro's "younger set," and Rebecca was obliged to make friends with the Robinson baby, he being the only long-clothes child in the village that winter. The faithful Seesaw had called at the side door of the brick house on the evening before his departure, and when Rebecca answered his knock, stammered solemnly, "Can I k-keep comp'ny with you when you g-g-row up?" "Certainly *not*," replied Rebecca, closing the door somewhat too speedily upon her precocious swain.

Mr. Simpson had come home in time to move his wife and children back to the town that had given them birth, a town by no means waiting with open arms to receive them. The Simpsons' moving was presided over by the village authori-

ties and somewhat anxiously watched by the entire neighborhood, but in spite of all precautions a pulpit chair, several
kerosene lamps, and a small stove disappeared from the
church and were successfully swapped in the course of Mr.
Simpson's driving tour from the old home to the new. It
gave Rebecca and Emma Jane some hours of sorrow to learn
that a certain village in the wake of Abner Simpson's line of
progress had acquired, through the medium of an ambitious young minister, a magnificent lamp for its new church
parlors. No money changed hands in the operation, for the
minister succeeded in getting the lamp in return for an old
bicycle. The only pleasant feature of the whole affair was
that Mr. Simpson, wholly unable to console his offspring
for the loss of the beloved object, mounted the bicycle and
rode away on it, not to be seen or heard of again for many a
long day.

The year was notable also as being the one in which Rebecca shot up like a young tree. She had seemingly never
grown an inch since she was ten years old, but once started
she attended to growing precisely as she did other things,
—with such energy that Miss Jane did nothing for months
but lengthen skirts, sleeves, and waists. In spite of all the
arts known to a thrifty New England woman, the limit of
letting down and piecing down was reached at last, and the
dresses were sent to Sunnybrook Farm to be made over for
Jenny.

There was another milestone, a sad one, marking a little
grave under a willow tree at Sunnybrook Farm. Mira, the
baby of the Randall family, died, and Rebecca went home
for a fortnight's visit. The sight of the small still shape that

had been Mira, the baby who had been her special charge ever since her birth, woke into being a host of new thoughts and wonderments; for it is sometimes the mystery of death that brings one to a consciousness of the still greater mystery of life.

It was a sorrowful home-coming for Rebecca. The death of Mira, the absence of John, who had been her special comrade, the sadness of her mother, the isolation of the little house, and the pinching economies that went on within it, all conspired to depress a child who was so sensitive to beauty and harmony as Rebecca.

Hannah seemed to have grown into a woman during Rebecca's absence. There had always been a strange unchild-like air about Hannah, but in certain ways she now appeared older than Aunt Jane—soberer, and more settled. She was pretty, though in a colorless fashion; pretty and capable.

Rebecca walked through all the old playgrounds and favorite haunts of her early childhood; all her familiar, her secret places; some of them known to John, some to herself alone. In the course of these lonely rambles she was ever thinking, thinking, of one subject. Hannah had never had a chance; never been freed from the daily care and work of the farm. She, Rebecca, had enjoyed all the privileges thus far. Life at the brick house had not been by any means a path of roses, but there had been comfort and the companionship of other children, as well as chances for study and reading. Riverboro had not been the world itself, but it had been a glimpse of it through a tiny peephole that was infinitely better than nothing. Rebecca shed more than one quiet tear before she could trust herself to offer up as a sacrifice that which she so much desired for herself. Then one morning as her visit neared its end she plunged into the subject boldly and said, "Hannah, after this term I'm going to stay at home and let you go away. Aunt Miranda has always wanted you, and it's only fair you should have your turn."

Hannah was darning stockings, and she threaded her needle and snipped off the yarn before she answered, "No, thank you, Becky. Mother couldn't do without me, and I hate going to school. I can read and write and cipher as well as anybody now, and that's enough for me. I'd die rather than teach school for a living. The winter'll go fast, for Will Melville is going to lend me his mother's sewing machine and I'm going to make white petticoats out of the piece of muslin Aunt Jane sent, and have 'em just solid with tucks. Then there's going to be a singing-school and a social circle in Temperance after New Year's, and I shall have a real good time now I'm grown up. I'm not one to be lonesome, Becky," Hannah ended with a blush; "I love this place."

Rebecca saw that she was speaking the truth, but she did not understand the blush till a year or two later.

Chapter Fifteen

Rebecca Represents the Family

There was another milestone; it was more than that, it was an "event"; an event that made a deep impression in several quarters and left a wake of smaller events in its train. This was the coming to Riverboro of the Reverend Amos Burch and wife, returned missionaries from Syria.

The Aid Society had called its meeting for a certain Wednesday in March of the year in which Rebecca ended her Riverboro school days and began her studies in Wareham. It was a raw, blustering day, snow on the ground, and a look in the sky of more to follow. Both Miranda and Jane had taken cold and decided that they could not leave the house in such weather, and this deflection from the path of duty worried Miranda, since she was an officer of the society. After making the breakfast table sufficiently uncomfortable and wishing plaintively that Jane wouldn't always insist on being sick at the same time she was, she decided that Rebecca must go to the meeting in their stead. "You'll be better than nobody, Rebecca," she said flatteringly; "your Aunt Jane shall write an excuse from afternoon school for you; you can wear your rubber boots and come home by the way of the meetin'-house. This Mr. Burch, if I remember right, used to know your Grandfather Sawyer, and stayed here once when he was candidatin'. He'll mebbe look for us there, and you must just go and represent the family, an' give him our respects. Be careful how you behave. Bow your head in prayer; sing all the hymns, but not too loud and bold; ask after Mis' Strout's boy; tell everybody what awful colds we've got; if you see a good chance, take your pocket handkerchief and wipe the dust off the melodeon before the meetin' begins, and get twenty-five cents out of the sittin'-room match-box in case there should be a collection."

Rebecca willingly assented. Anything interested her, even a village missionary meeting, and the idea of representing the family was rather intoxicating.

The service was held in the Sunday-School room, and although the Reverend Mr. Burch was on the platform when Rebecca entered, there were only a dozen persons present. Feeling a little shy and considerably too young for this assemblage, Rebecca sought the shelter of a friendly face, and seeing Mrs. Robinson in one of the side seats near the front, she walked up the aisle and sat beside her.

"Both my aunts had bad colds," she said softly, "and sent me to represent the family."

"That's Mrs. Burch on the platform with her husband," whispered Mrs. Robinson. "She's awful tanned up, ain't she? If you're goin' to save souls seems like you hev' to part with your complexion. Eudoxy Morton ain't come yet; I

hope to the land she will, or Mis' Deacon Milliken'll pitch
the tunes where we can't reach 'em with a ladder; can't you
pitch, afore she gits her breath and clears her throat?"

Mrs. Burch was a slim, frail little woman with dark hair,
a broad low forehead, and patient mouth. She was dressed
in a well-worn black silk, and looked so tired that Rebecca's
heart went out to her.

"They're poor as Job's turkey," whispered Mrs. Robinson;
"but if you give 'em anything they'd turn right round and
give it to the heathen. His congregation up to Parsonsfield
clubbed together and give him that gold watch he carries;
I s'pose he'd 'a' handed that over too, only heathens always
tell time by the sun 'n' don't need watches. Eudoxy ain't
comin'; now for massy's sake, Rebecca, do git ahead of Mis'
Deacon Milliken and pitch real low."

The meeting began with prayer and then the Reverend
Mr. Burch announced, to the tune of "Mendon":

> Church of our God! arise and shine,
> Bright with the beams of truth divine:
> Then shall thy radiance stream afar,
> Wide as the heathen nations are.
>
> Gentiles and kings thy light shall view,
> And shall admire and love thee too;
> They come, like clouds across the sky,
> As doves that to their windows fly.

"Is there anyone present who will assist us at the instru-
ment?" he asked unexpectedly.

Everybody looked at everybody else, and nobody moved;
then there came a voice out of a far corner saying in-
formally, "Rebecca, why don't you?" It was Mrs. Cobb. Re-

becca could have played "Mendon" in the dark, so she went
to the melodeon and did so without any ado, no member
of her family being present to give her self-consciousness.

The talk that ensued was much the usual sort of thing.
Mr. Burch made impassioned appeals for the spreading of
the gospel, and added his entreaties that all who were prevented from visiting in person the peoples who sat in darkness should contribute liberally to the support of others who
could. But he did more than this. He was a pleasant, earnest
speaker, and he interwove his discourse with stories of life
in a foreign land,—of the manners, the customs, the speech,
the point of view; even giving glimpses of the daily round,
the common task, of his own household, the work of his devoted helpmate and their little group of children, all born
under Syrian skies.

Rebecca sat entranced, having been given the key of another world. Riverboro had faded; the Sunday-School room,
with Mrs. Robinson's red plaid shawl, and Deacon Milliken's wig, on crooked, the bare benches and torn hymn-
books, the hanging texts and maps, were no longer visible,
and she saw blue skies· and burning stars, white turbans
and gay colors; Mr. Burch had not said so, but perhaps
there were mosques and temples and minarets and date-
palms. What stories they must know, those children born
under Syrian skies! Then she was called upon to play "Jesus
shall reign where'er the sun."

The contribution box was passed and Mr. Burch prayed.
As he opened his eyes and gave out the last hymn he looked
at the handful of people, at the scattered pennies and dimes
in the contribution box, and reflected that his mission was

not only to gather funds for the building of his church, but
to keep alive, in all these remote and lonely neighborhoods,
that love for the cause which was its only hope in the years
to come.

"If any of the sisters will provide entertainment," he said,
"Mrs. Burch and I will remain among you to-night and to-
morrow. In that event we could hold a parlor meeting. My
wife and one of my children would wear the native costume,
we would display some specimens of Syrian handiwork, and
give an account of our educational methods with the children. These informal parlor meetings, admitting of questions or conversation, are often the means of interesting
those not commonly found at church services; so I repeat,
if any member of the congregation desires it and offers
her hospitality, we will gladly stay and tell you more of the
Lord's work."

A pall of silence settled over the little assembly. There
was some cogent reason why every "sister" there was dis-
inclined for company. Some had no spare room, some had a
larder less well stocked than usual, some had sickness in the
family, some were "unequally yoked together with unbe-
lievers" who disliked strange ministers. Mrs. Burch's thin
hands fingered her black silk nervously. "Would no one
speak!" thought Rebecca, her heart fluttering with sympathy. Mrs. Robinson leaned over and whispered signifi-
cantly, "The missionaries always used to be entertained at
the brick house; your grandfather never would let 'em sleep
anywheres else when he was alive." She meant this for a
stab at Miss Miranda's parsimony, remembering the four
spare chambers, closed from January to December; but Re-

becca thought it was intended as a suggestion. If it had been a former custom, perhaps her aunts would want her to do the right thing; for what else was she representing the family? So, delighted that duty lay in so pleasant a direction, she rose from her seat and said in a pretty voice and with the quaint manner that so separated her from all the other young people in the village, "My aunts, Miss Miranda and Miss Jane Sawyer, would be very happy to have you visit them at the brick house, as the ministers always used to do when their father was alive. They sent their respects by me." The "respects" might have been the freedom of the city, or an equestrian statue, when presented in this way, and the aunts would have shuddered could they have foreseen the manner of delivery; but it was vastly impressive to the audience, who concluded that Mirandy Sawyer must be making her way uncommonly fast to mansions in the skies, else what meant this abrupt change of heart?

Mr. Burch bowed courteously, accepted the invitation "in the same spirit in which it was offered," and asked Brother Milliken to lead in prayer.

If the Eternal Ear could ever tire it would have ceased long ere this to listen to Deacon Milliken, who had wafted to the throne of grace the same prayer, with very slight variations, for forty years. Mrs. Perkins followed; she had several petitions at her command, good sincere ones too, but a little cut and dried, made of Scripture texts laboriously woven together. Rebecca wondered why she always ended, at the most peaceful seasons, with the form, "Do Thou be with us, God of Battles, while we strive onward like Christian soldiers marching as to war." But everything sounded real to her to-day; she was in a devout mood, and many things Mr. Burch had said had moved her strangely. As she lifted her head the minister looked directly at her and said, "Will our young sister close the service by leading us in prayer?"

Every drop of blood in Rebecca's body seemed to stand still, and her heart almost stopped beating. Mrs. Cobb's excited breathing could be heard distinctly in the silence. There was nothing extraordinary in Mr. Burch's request. In his journeyings among country congregations he was constantly in the habit of meeting young members who had "experienced religion" and joined the church when nine or ten years old. Rebecca was now thirteen; she had played the melodeon, led the singing, delivered her aunts' invitation with an air of great worldly wisdom, and he, concluding that she must be a youthful pillar of the church, called upon her with the utmost simplicity.

Rebecca's plight was pathetic. How could she refuse; how could she explain she was not a "member"; how could she pray before all those elderly women! John Rogers at the stake hardly suffered more than this poor child for the moment as she rose to her feet, forgetting that ladies prayed sitting, while deacons stood in prayer. Her mind was a maze of pictures that the Reverend Mr. Burch had flung on the screen. She knew the conventional phraseology, of course; what New England child, accustomed to Wednesday evening meetings, does not? But her own secret prayers were different. However, she began slowly and tremulously:—

"Our Father who art in Heaven, . . . Thou art God in

Syria just the same as in Maine; . . . over there to-day are blue skies and yellow stars and burning suns . . . the great trees are waving in the warm air, while here the snow lies thick under our feet, . . . but no distance is too far for God to travel and so He is with us here as He is with them there, . . . and our thoughts rise to Him 'as doves that to their windows fly.' . . .

"We cannot all be missionaries, teaching people to be good, . . . some of us have not learned yet how to be good ourselves, but if thy kingdom is to come and thy will is to be done on earth as it is in heaven, everybody must try and everybody must help, . . . those who are old and tired and those who are young and strong. . . . The little children of whom we have heard, those born under Syrian skies, have strange and interesting work to do for Thee, and some of us would like to travel in far lands and do wonderful brave things for the heathen and gently take away their idols of wood and stone. But perhaps we have to stay at home and do what is given us to do . . . sometimes even things we dislike, . . . but that must be what it means in the hymn we sang, when it talked about the sweet perfume that rises with every morning sacrifice. . . . This is the way that God teaches us to be meek and patient, and the thought that He has willed it so should rob us of our fears and help us bear the years. Amen."

The "Amen" said, she sat down, or presumed she sat down, on what she believed to be a bench, and there was a benediction. In a moment or two, when the room ceased spinning, she went up to Mrs. Burch, who kissed her affectionately and said, "My dear, how glad I am that we are

going to stay with you. Will half-past five be too late for us
to come? It is three now, and we have to go to the station
for our valise and for our children. We left them there, being uncertain whether we should go back or stop here."

Rebecca said that half-past five was their supper hour,
and then accepted an invitation to drive home with Mrs.
Cobb. Her face was flushed and her lip quivered in a way
that Aunt Sarah had learned to know, so the homeward
drive was taken almost in silence. The bleak wind and Aunt
Sarah's quieting presence brought her back to herself, however, and she entered the brick house cheerily. Being too
full of news to wait in the side entry to take off her rubber
boots, she carefully lifted a braided rug into the sitting-
room and stood on that while she removed her boots.

"There are your shoes warming by the fire," said Aunt
Jane. "Slip them right on while you talk."

Chapter Sixteen

Deacon Israel's Successor

It was a very small meeting, Aunt Miranda," began Rebecca, "and the missionary and his wife are lovely people, and they are coming here to stay all night and to-morrow with you. I hope you won't mind."

"Coming here!" exclaimed Miranda, letting her knitting fall in her lap, and taking her spectacles off, as she always did in moments of extreme excitement. "Did they invite themselves?"

"No," Rebecca answered. "I had to invite them for you; but I thought you'd like to have such interesting company. It was this way—"

"Stop your explainin', and tell me first when they'll be here. Right away?"

"No, not for two hours—about half-past five."

"Then you can explain, if you can, who gave you authority to invite a passel of strangers to stop here overnight, when you know we ain't had any company for twenty years, and don't intend to have any for another twenty,—or at any rate, while I'm the head of the house."

"Don't blame her, Miranda, till you've heard her story," said Jane. "It was in my mind right along, if we went to the meeting, some such thing might happen, on account of Mr. Burch knowing father."

"The meeting was a small one," began Rebecca. "I gave all your messages, and everybody was disappointed you couldn't come, for the president wasn't there, and Mrs. Matthews took the chair, which was a pity, for the seat wasn't nearly big enough for her, and she reminded me of a line in a hymn we sang, 'Wide as the heathen nations are,' and she wore that kind of a beaver garden-hat that always gets on one side. And Mr. Burch talked beautifully about the Syrian heathen, and the singing went real well, and there looked to be about forty cents in the basket that was passed on our side. And that wouldn't save even a heathen baby, would it? Then Mr. Burch said, if any sister would offer entertainment, they would pass the night, and have a parlor meeting in Riverboro to-morrow, with Mrs. Burch in Syrian costume, and lovely foreign things to show. Then he waited and waited, and nobody said a word. I was so mortified I didn't know what to do. And then he repeated what he said, and explained why he wanted to stay, and you could see he thought it was his duty. Just then Mrs. Robinson whispered to me and said the missionaries always used to go to the brick house when grandfather was alive, and that he never would let them sleep anywhere else. I didn't know you had stopped having them, because no traveling ministers have been here, except just for a Sunday morning, since I came to Riverboro. So I thought I ought to invite them as you weren't there to do it for yourself, and you told me to represent the family."

"What did you do—go up and introduce yourself as folks was goin' out?"

"No; I stood right up in meeting. I had to, for Mr. Burch's feelings were getting hurt at nobody's speaking. So I said, 'My aunts, Miss Miranda and Miss Jane Sawyer, would be happy to have you visit at the brick house, just as the missionaries always did when their father was alive, and they sent their respects by me.' Then I sat down; and Mr. Burch prayed for grandfather, and called him a man of God, and thanked our Heavenly Father that his spirit was still alive in his descendants (that was you), and that the good old house where so many of the brethren had been cheered and helped, and from which so many had gone out strengthened for the fight, was still hospitably open for the stranger and wayfarer."

Sometimes, when the heavenly bodies are in just the right conjunction, nature seems to be the most perfect art. The word or the deed coming straight from the heart, without any thought of effect, seems inspired.

A certain gateway in Miranda Sawyer's soul had been closed for years; not all at once had it been done, but gradually, and without her full knowledge. If Rebecca had plotted for days, and with the utmost cunning, she could not have effected an entrance into that forbidden country, and now, unknown to both of them, the gate swung on its stiff and rusty hinges, and the favoring wind of opportunity opened it wider and wider as time went on. All things had worked together amazingly for good. The memory of old days had been evoked, and the daily life of a pious and venerated father called to mind; the Sawyer name had been publicly dignified and praised; Rebecca had comported herself as the granddaughter of Deacon Israel Sawyer should, and showed conclusively that she was not "all Randall," as had been supposed. Miranda was rather mollified by and pleased with the turn of events, although she did not intend to show it, or give anybody any reason to expect that this expression of hospitality was to serve for a precedent on any subsequent occasion.

"Well, I see you did only what you was obliged to do, Rebecca," she said, "and you worded your invitation as nice as anybody could have done. I wish your Aunt Jane and me wasn't both so worthless with these colds; but it only shows the good of havin' a clean house, with every room in order, whether open or shut, and enough victuals cooked so you can't be surprised and belittled by anybody, whatever happens. There was half a dozen there that might have entertained the Burches as easy as not, if they hadn't 'a' been too mean or lazy. Why didn't your missionaries come right along with you?"

"They had to go to the station for their valise and their children."

"Are there children?" groaned Miranda.

"Yes, Aunt Miranda, all born under Syrian skies."

"Syrian grandmother!" ejaculated Miranda (and it was not a fact). "How many?"

"I didn't think to ask; but I will get two rooms ready, and if there are any over I'll take 'em into my bed," said Rebecca, secretly hoping that this would be the case. "Now, as you're both half sick, couldn't you trust me just once to get ready for the company? You can come up when I call. Will you?"

"I believe I will," sighed Miranda reluctantly. "I'll lay down side o' Jane in our bedroom and see if I can get strength to cook supper. It's half-past three—don't you let me lay a minute past five. I kep' a good fire in the kitchen stove. I don't know, I'm sure, why I should have baked a pot o' beans in the middle of the week, but they'll come in handy. Father used to say there was nothing that went right to the spot with returned missionaries like pork 'n' beans 'n' brown bread. Fix up the two south chambers, Rebecca."

Rebecca, given a free hand for the only time in her life, dashed upstairs like a whirlwind. Every room in the brick house was as neat as wax, and she had only to pull up the shades, go over the floors with a whisk broom, and dust the furniture. The aunts could hear her scurrying to and fro, beating up pillows and feather beds, flapping towels, jingling crockery, singing meanwhile in her clear voice:—

> In vain with lavish kindness
>   The gifts of God are strown;
> The heathen in his blindness
>   Bows down to wood and stone.

She had grown to be a handy little creature, and tasks she was capable of doing at all she did like a flash, so that when she called her aunts at five o'clock to pass judgment, she had accomplished wonders. There were fresh towels on bureaus and washstands, the beds were fair and smooth, the pitchers were filled, and soap and matches were laid out; newspaper, kindling, and wood were in the boxes, and a large stick burned slowly in each air-tight stove. "I thought I'd better just take the chill off," she explained, "as they're right from Syria; and that reminds me, I must look it up in the geography before they get here."

There was nothing to disapprove, so the two sisters went downstairs to make some slight changes in their dress. As they passed the parlor door Miranda thought she heard a crackle and looked in. The shades were up, there was a cheerful blaze in the open stove in the front parlor, and a fire laid on the hearth in the back room. Rebecca's own lamp, her second Christmas present from Mr. Aladdin, stood on a marble-topped table in the corner, the light that came softly through its rose-colored shade transforming the stiff and gloomy ugliness of the room into a place where one could sit and love one's neighbor.

"For massy's sake, Rebecca," called Miss Miranda up the stairs, "did you think we'd better open the parlor?"

Rebecca came out on the landing braiding her hair.

"We did on Thanksgiving and Christmas, and I thought this was about as great an occasion," she said. "I moved the wax flowers off the mantelpiece so they wouldn't melt, and put the shells, the coral, and the green stuffed bird on top of the what-not, so the children wouldn't ask to play with them. Brother Milliken's coming over to see Mr. Burch about business, and I shouldn't wonder if Brother and Sister Cobb happened in. Don't go down cellar, I'll be there in a minute to do the running."

Miranda and Jane exchanged glances.

"Ain't she the beatin'est creetur that ever was born int'

the world!" exclaimed Miranda; "but she can turn off work when she's got a mind to!"

At quarter-past five everything was ready, and the neighbors, those at least who were within sight of the brick house (a prominent object in the landscape when there were no leaves on the trees), were curious almost to desperation. Shades up in both parlors! Shades up in the two south bed rooms! And fires—if human vision was to be relied on—fires in about every room. If it had not been for the kind offices of a lady who had been at the meeting, and who charitably called in at one or two houses and explained the reason of all this preparation, there would have been no sleep in many families.

The missionary party arrived promptly, and there were but two children, seven or eight having been left with the brethren in Portland, to diminish traveling expenses. Jane escorted them all upstairs, while Miranda watched the cooking of the supper; but Rebecca promptly took the two little girls away from their mother, divested them of their wraps, smoothed their hair, and brought them down to the kitchen to smell the beans.

There was a bountiful supper, and the presence of the young people robbed it of all possible stiffness. Aunt Jane helped clear the table and put away the food, while Miranda entertained in the parlor; but Rebecca and the infant Burches washed the dishes and held high carnival in the kitchen, doing only trifling damage—breaking a cup and plate that had been cracked before, emptying a silver spoon with some dishwater out of the back door (an act never permitted at the brick house), and putting coffee grounds in the sink. All evidences of crime having been removed by Rebecca, and damages repaired in all possible cases, the three entered the parlor, where Mr. and Mrs. Cobb and Deacon and Mrs. Milliken had already appeared.

It was such a pleasant evening! Occasionally they left the heathen in his blindness bowing down to wood and stone, not for long, but just to give themselves (and him) time enough to breathe, and then the Burches told strange, beautiful, marvelous things. The two smaller children sang together, and Rebecca, at the urgent request of Mrs. Burch, seated herself at the tinkling old piano and gave "Wild roved an Indian girl, bright Alfarata" with considerable spirit and style.

At eight o'clock she crossed the room, handed a palm-leaf fan to her Aunt Miranda, ostensibly that she might shade her eyes from the lamplight; but it was a piece of strategy that gave her an opportunity to whisper, "How about cookies?"

"Do you think it's worth while?" sibilated Miss Miranda in answer.

"The Perkinses always do."

"All right. You know where they be."

Rebecca moved quietly towards the door, and the young Burches rushed after her as if they could not bear a second's separation. In five minutes they returned, the little ones bearing plates of thin caraway wafers,—hearts, diamonds, and circles daintily sugared, and flecked with caraway seed raised in the garden behind the house. These were a specialty of Miss Jane's, and Rebecca carried a tray with six tiny crystal glasses filled with dandelion wine, for which

Miss Miranda had been famous in years gone by. Old Deacon Israel had always had it passed, and he had bought the glasses himself in Boston. Miranda admired them greatly, not only for their beauty but because they held so little. Before their advent the dandelion wine had been served in sherry glasses.

As soon as these refreshments—commonly called a "*colation*" in Riverboro—had been genteelly partaken of, Rebecca looked at the clock, rose from her chair in the children's corner, and said cheerfully, "Come! time for little missionaries to be in bed!"

Everybody laughed at this, the big missionaries most of all, as the young people shook hands and disappeared with Rebecca.

Chapter Seventeen

A Change of Heart

That niece of yours is the most remarkable girl I have seen in years," said Mr. Burch when the door closed.

"She seems to be turnin' out smart enough lately, but she's consid'able heedless," answered Miranda, "an' 'most too lively."

"We must remember that it is deficient, not excessive vitality, that makes the greatest trouble in this world," returned Mr. Burch.

"She'd make a wonderful missionary," said Mrs. Burch; "with her voice, and her magnetism, and her gift of language."

"If I was to say which of the two she was best adapted for, I'd say she'd make a better heathen," remarked Miranda curtly.

"My sister don't believe in flattering children," hastily interpolated Jane, glancing toward Mrs. Burch, who seemed somewhat shocked, and was about to open her lips to ask if Rebecca was not a "professor."

Mrs. Cobb had been looking for this question all the evening and dreading some allusion to her favorite as gifted·in prayer. She had taken an instantaneous and illogical dislike to the Reverend Mr. Burch in the afternoon because he called upon Rebecca to "lead." She had seen the pallor creep into the girl's face, the hunted look in her eyes, and the trembling of the lashes on her cheeks, and realized the ordeal through which she was passing. Her prejudice against the minister had relaxed under his genial talk and presence, but feeling that Mrs. Burch was about to tread on dangerous ground, she hastily asked her if one had to change cars many times going from Riverboro to Syria. She felt that it was not a particularly appropriate question, but it served her turn.

Deacon Milliken, meantime, said to Miss Sawyer, "Mirandy, do you know who Rebecky reminds me of?"

"I can guess pretty well," she replied.

"Then you've noticed it too! I thought at first, seein' she favored her father so on the outside, that she was the same all through; but she ain't, she's like your father, Israel Sawyer."

"I don't see how you make that out," said Miranda, thoroughly astonished.

"It struck me this afternoon when she got up to give your invitation in meetin'. It was kind o' cur'ous, but she set in the same seat he used to when he was leader o' the Sabbath-School. You know his old way of holding his chin up and throwin' his head back a leetle when he got up to say something? Well, she done the very same thing; there was more'n one spoke of it."

The callers left before nine, and at that hour (an impos-

sibly dissipated one for the brick house) the family retired
for the night. As Rebecca carried Mrs. Burch's candle upstairs and found herself thus alone with her for a minute,
she said shyly, "Will you please tell Mr. Burch that I'm not
a member of the church? I didn't know what to do when he
asked me to pray this afternoon. I hadn't the courage to say
I had never done it out loud and didn't know how. I
couldn't think; and I was so frightened I wanted to sink into
the floor. It seemed bold and wicked for me to pray before
all those old church members and make believe I was better
than I really was; but then again, wouldn't God think I was
wicked not to be willing to pray when a minister asked me
to?"

The candlelight fell on Rebecca's flushed, sensitive face.
Mrs. Burch bent and kissed her good-night. "Don't be
troubled," she said. "I'll tell Mr. Burch, and I guess God will
understand."

Rebecca waked before six the next morning, so full of
household cares that sleep was impossible. She went to the
window and looked out; it was still dark, and a blustering,
boisterous day.

"Aunt Jane told me she would get up at half-past six and
have breakfast at half-past seven," she thought; "but I dare
say they are both sick with their colds, and Aunt Miranda
will be fidgety with so many in the house. I believe I'll creep
down and start things for a surprise."

She put on a wadded wrapper and slippers and stole
quietly down the tabooed front stairs, carefully closed the
kitchen door behind her so that no noise should waken the

rest of the household, busied herself for a half-hour with the early morning routine she knew so well, and then went back to her room to dress before calling the children.

Contrary to expectation, Miss Jane, who the evening before felt better than Miranda, grew worse in the night, and was wholly unable to leave her bed in the morning. Miranda grumbled without ceasing during the progress of her hasty toilet, blaming everybody in the universe for the afflictions she had borne and was to bear during the day; she even castigated the Missionary Board that had sent the Burches to Syria, and gave it as her unbiased opinion that those who went to foreign lands for the purpose of saving heathen should stay there and save 'em, and not go gallivantin' all over the earth with a passel o' children, visitin' folks that didn't want 'em and never asked 'em.

Jane lay anxiously and restlessly in bed with a feverish headache, wondering how her sister could manage without her.

Miranda walked stiffly through the dining-room, tying a shawl over her head to keep the draughts away, intending to start the breakfast fire and then call Rebecca down, set her to work, and tell her, meanwhile, a few plain facts concerning the proper way of representing the family at a missionary meeting.

She opened the kitchen door and stared vaguely about her, wondering whether she had strayed into the wrong house by mistake.

The shades were up, and there was a roaring fire in the stove; the teakettle was singing and bubbling as it sent out a cloud of steam, and pushed over its capacious nose was a half-sheet of note paper with "Compliments of Rebecca" scrawled on it. The coffee pot was scalding, the coffee was measured out in a bowl, and broken eggshells for the settling process were standing near. The cold potatoes and corned beef were in the wooden tray, and "Regards of Rebecca" stuck on the chopping-knife. The brown loaf was out, the white loaf was out, the toast rack was out, the doughnuts were out, the milk was skimmed, the butter had been brought from the dairy.

Miranda removed the shawl from her head and sank into the kitchen rocker, ejaculating under her breath, "She is the beatin'est child! I declare she's all Sawyer!"

The day and the evening passed off with credit and honor to everybody concerned, even to Jane, who had the discretion to recover instead of growing worse and acting as a damper to the general enjoyment. The Burches left with lively regrets, and the little missionaries, bathed in tears, swore eternal friendship with Rebecca, who pressed into their hands at parting a poem composed before breakfast.

TO MARY AND MARTHA BURCH

Born under Syrian skies,
   'Neath hotter suns than ours;
The children grew and bloomed,
   Like little tropic flowers.

When they first saw the light,
   'T was in a heathen land.
Not Greenland's icy mountains,
   Nor India's coral strand,

But some mysterious country
   Where men are nearly black

> And where of true religion,
> There is a painful lack.
>
> Then let us haste in helping
> The Missionary Board
> Seek dark-skinned unbelievers,
> And teach them of their Lord.
>
> REBECCA ROWENA RANDALL.

It can readily be seen that this visit of the returned missionaries to Riverboro was not without somewhat far-reaching results. Mr. and Mrs. Burch themselves looked back upon it as one of the rarest pleasures of their half year at home. The neighborhood extracted considerable eager conversation from it; argument, rebuttal, suspicion, certainty, retrospect, and prophecy. Deacon Milliken gave ten dollars towards the conversion of Syria to Congregationalism, and Mrs. Milliken had a spell of sickness over her husband's rash generosity.

It would be pleasant to state that Miranda Sawyer was an entirely changed woman afterwards, but that is not the fact. The tree that has been getting a twist for twenty years cannot be straightened in the twinkling of an eye. It is certain, however, that although the difference to the outward eye was very small, it nevertheless existed, and she was less censorious in her treatment of Rebecca, less harsh in her judgments, more hopeful of final salvation for her. This had come about largely from her sudden vision that Rebecca, after all, inherited something from the Sawyer side of the house instead of belonging, mind, body, and soul, to the despised Randall stock. Everything that was interesting in Rebecca, and every evidence of power, capability, or talent afterwards displayed by her, Miranda ascribed to the brick house training, and this gave her a feeling of honest pride, the pride of a master workman who has built success out of the most unpromising material; but never, to the very end, even when the waning of her bodily strength relaxed her iron grip and weakened her power of repression, never once did she show that pride or make a single demonstration of affection.

Poor misplaced, belittled Lorenzo de Medici Randall, thought ridiculous and good-for-naught by his associates, because he resembled them in nothing! If Riverboro could have been suddenly emptied into a larger community, with different and more flexible opinions, he was, perhaps, the only personage in the entire population who would have attracted the smallest attention. It was fortunate for his daughter that she had been dowered with a little practical ability from her mother's family, but if Lorenzo had never done anything else in the world, he might have glorified himself that he had prevented Rebecca from being all Sawyer. Failure as he was, complete and entire, he had generously handed down to her all that was best in himself, and prudently retained all that was unworthy. Few fathers are capable of such delicate discrimination.

The brick house did not speedily become a sort of wayside inn, a place of innocent revelry and joyous welcome; but the missionary company was an entering wedge, and Miranda allowed one spare bed to be made up "in case anything should happen," while the crystal glasses were kept on the second from the top, instead of the top shelf, in the china closet. Rebecca had had to stand on a chair to reach them; now she could do it by stretching; and this is symbolic of the way in which she unconsciously scaled the walls of Miss Miranda's dogmatism and prejudice.

Miranda went so far as to say that she wouldn't mind if the Burches came every once in a while, but she was afraid he'd spread abroad the fact of his visit, and missionaries' families would be underfoot the whole continual time. As a case in point, she gracefully cited the fact that if a tramp got a good meal at anybody's back door, 't was said that he'd leave some kind of a sign so that all other tramps would know where they were likely to receive the same treatment.

It is to be feared that there is some truth in this homely illustration, and Miss Miranda's dread as to her future responsibilities had some foundation, though not of the precise sort she had in mind. The soul grows into lovely habits as easily as into ugly ones, and the moment a life begins to blossom into beautiful words and deeds, that moment a new standard of conduct is established, and your eager neighbors look to you for a continuous manifestation of the good cheer, the sympathy, the ready wit, the comradeship, or the inspiration, you once showed yourself capable of. Bear figs for a season or two, and the world outside the orchard is very unwilling you should bear thistles.

The effect of the Burches' visit on Rebecca is not easily described. Nevertheless, as she looked back upon it from the vantage ground of after years, she felt that the moment when Mr. Burch asked her to "lead in prayer" marked an epoch in her life.

If you have ever observed how courteous and gracious and mannerly you feel when you don a beautiful new frock;

if you have ever noticed the feeling of reverence stealing over you when you close your eyes, clasp your hands, and bow your head; if you have ever watched your sense of repulsion toward a fellow creature melt a little under the exercise of daily politeness, you may understand how the adoption of the outward and visible sign has some strange influence in developing the inward and spiritual state of which it is the expression.

It is only when one has grown old and dull that the soul is heavy and refuses to rise. The young soul is ever winged; a breath stirs it to an upward flight. Rebecca was asked to bear witness to a state of mind or feeling of whose existence she had only the vaguest consciousness. She obeyed, and as she uttered words they became true in the uttering; as she voiced aspirations they settled into realities.

As "dove that to its window flies," her spirit soared towards a great light, dimly discovered at first, but brighter as she came closer to it. To become sensible of oneness with the Divine heart before any sense of separation has been felt, this is surely the most beautiful way for the child to find God.

Chapter Eighteen

The Sky-line Widens

The time so long and eagerly waited for had come, and Rebecca was a student at Wareham. Persons who had enjoyed the social bewilderments and advantages of foreign courts, or had mingled freely in the intellectual circles of great universities, might not have looked upon Wareham as an extraordinary experience; but it was as much of an advance upon Riverboro as that village had been upon Sunnybrook Farm. Rebecca's intention was to complete the four years' course in three, as it was felt by the parties concerned that when she had attained the ripe age of seventeen she must be ready to earn her own living and help in the education of the younger children. While she was wondering how this could be successfully accomplished, some of the other girls were cogitating as to how they could meander through the four years and come out at the end knowing no more than at the beginning. This would seem a difficult, well-nigh an impossible task, but it can be achieved, and has been, at other seats of learning than modest little Wareham.

Rebecca was to go to the fro on the cars daily from September to Christmas, and then board in Wareham during the three coldest months. Emma Jane's parents had always thought that a year or two in the Edgewood High School (three miles from Riverboro) would serve every purpose for their daughter and send her into the world with as fine an intellectual polish as she could well sustain. Emma Jane had hitherto heartily concurred in this opinion, for if there was any one thing that she detested it was the learning of lessons. One book was as bad as another in her eyes, and she could have seen the libraries of the world sinking into ocean depths and have eaten her dinner cheerfully the while; but matters assumed a different complexion when she was sent to Edgewood and Rebecca to Wareham. She bore it for a week—seven endless days of absence from the beloved object, whom she could see only in the evenings when both were busy with their lessons. Sunday offered an opportunity to put the matter before her father, who proved obdurate. He didn't believe in education and thought she had full enough already. He never intended to keep up "blacksmithing" for good when he leased his farm and came into Riverboro, but proposed to go back to it presently, and by that time Emma Jane would have finished school and would be ready to help her mother with the dairy work.

Another week passed. Emma Jane pined visibly and audibly. Her color faded, and her appetite (at table) dwindled almost to nothing.

Her mother alluded plaintively to the fact that the Perkinses had a habit of going into declines; that she'd always feared that Emma Jane's complexion was too beautiful to be healthy; that some men would be proud of having an ambitious daughter, and be glad to give her the best advantages; that she feared the daily journeys to Edgewood were going to be too much for her own health, and Mr. Perkins would have to hire a boy to drive Emma Jane; and finally that when a girl had such a passion for learning as Emma Jane, it seemed almost like wickedness to cross her will.

Mr. Perkins bore this for several days until his temper, digestion, and appetite were all sensibly affected; then he bowed his head to the inevitable, and Emma Jane flew, like a captive set free, to the loved one's bower. Neither did her courage flag, although it was put to terrific tests when she entered the academic groves of Wareham. She passed in only two subjects, but went cheerfully into the preparatory department with her five "conditions," intending to let the stream of education play gently over her mental surfaces and not get any wetter than she could help. It is not possible to blink the truth that Emma Jane was dull; but a dogged, unswerving loyalty, and the gift of devoted, unselfish loving, these, after all, are talents of a sort, and may possibly be of as much value in the world as a sense of numbers or a faculty for languages.

Wareham was a pretty village with a broad main street shaded by great maples and elms. It had an apothecary, a blacksmith, a plumber, several shops of one sort and another, two churches, and many boarding-houses; but all its interests gathered about its seminary and its academy. These seats of learning were neither better nor worse than others of their kind, but differed much in efficiency, according as the principal who chanced to be at the head was a man of

power and inspiration or the reverse. There were boys and
girls gathered from all parts of the county and state, and
they were of every kind and degree as to birth, position in
the world, wealth or poverty. There was an opportunity for
a deal of foolish and imprudent behavior, but on the whole
surprisingly little advantage was taken of it. Among the
third and fourth year students there was a certain amount of
going to and from the trains in couples; some carrying of
heavy books up the hill by the sterner sex for their feminine
schoolmates, and occasional bursts of silliness on the part
of heedless and precocious girls, among whom was Huldah
Meserve. She was friendly enough with Emma Jane and
Rebecca, but grew less and less intimate as time went on.
She was extremely pretty, with a profusion of auburn hair,
and a few very tiny freckles, to which she constantly alluded, as no one could possibly detect them without noting
her porcelain skin and her curling lashes. She had merry
eyes, a somewhat too plump figure for her years, and was
popularly supposed to have a fascinating way with her.
Riverboro being poorly furnished with beaux, she intended
to have as good a time during her four years at Wareham as
circumstances would permit. Her idea of pleasure was an
ever-changing circle of admirers to fetch and carry for her,
the more publicly the better; incessant chaff and laughter
and vivacious conversation, made eloquent and effective
by arch looks and telling glances. She had a habit of confiding her conquests to less fortunate girls and bewailing the
incessant havoc and damage she was doing; a damage she
avowed herself as innocent of, in intention, as any new-born

lamb. It does not take much of this sort of thing to wreck
an ordinary friendship, so before long Rebecca and Emma
Jane sat in one end of the railway train in going to and from
Riverboro, and Huldah occupied the other with her court.
Sometimes this was brilliant beyond words, including a certain youthful Monte Cristo, who on Fridays expended thirty
cents on a round-trip ticket and traveled from Wareham
to Riverboro merely to be near Huldah; sometimes, too, the
circle was reduced to the popcorn-and-peanut boy of the
train, who seemed to serve every purpose in default of better game.

Rebecca was in the normally unconscious state that belonged to her years; boys were good comrades, but no more;
she liked reciting in the same class with them, everything
seemed to move better; but from vulgar and precocious
flirtations she was protected by her ideals. There was little
in the lads she had met thus far to awaken her fancy, for it
habitually fed on better meat. Huldah's schoolgirl ro-
mances, with their wealth of commonplace detail, were not
the stuff her dreams were made of, when dreams did flutter
across the sensitive plate of her mind.

Among the teachers at Wareham was one who influenced
Rebecca profoundly, Miss Emily Maxwell, with whom she
studied English literature and composition. Miss Maxwell,
as the niece of one of Maine's ex-governors and the daughter of one of Bowdoin's professors, was the most remarkable
personality in Wareham, and that her few years of teaching
happened to be in Rebecca's time was the happiest of all
chances. There was no indecision or delay in the establish-

ment of their relations; Rebecca's heart flew like an arrow to
its mark, and her mind, meeting its superior, settled at once
into an abiding attitude of respectful homage.

It was rumored that Miss Maxwell "wrote," which word,
when uttered in a certain tone, was understood to mean not
that a person had command of penmanship, Spencerian or
otherwise, but that she had appeared in print.

"You'll like her; she writes," whispered Huldah to Rebecca
the first morning at prayers, where the faculty sat in an im-
posing row on the front seats. "She writes; and I call her
stuck up."

Nobody seemed possessed of exact information with
which to satisfy the hungry mind, but there was believed to
be at least one person in existence who had seen, with his
own eyes, an essay by Miss Maxwell in a magazine. This
height of achievement made Rebecca somewhat shy of her,
but she looked her admiration; something that most of the
class could never do with the unsatisfactory organs of vision
given them by Mother Nature. Miss Maxwell's glance was
always meeting a pair of eager dark eyes; when she said
anything particularly good, she looked for approval to the
corner of the second bench, where every shade of feeling
she wished to evoke was reflected on a certain sensitive
young face.

One day, when the first essay of the class was under discussion, she asked each new pupil to bring her some composition written during the year before, that she might
judge the work, and know precisely with what material she
had to deal. Rebecca lingered after the others, and approached the desk shyly.

"I haven't any compositions here, Miss Maxwell, but I can find one when I go home on Friday. They are packed away in a box in the attic."

"Carefully tied with pink and blue ribbons?" asked Miss Maxwell, with a whimsical smile.

"No," answered Rebecca, shaking her head decidedly; "I wanted to use ribbons, because all the other girls did, and they looked so pretty, but I used to tie my essays with twine strings on purpose; and the one on 'Solitude' I fastened with an old shoelacing just to show it what I thought of it!"

" 'Solitude'!" laughed Miss Maxwell, raising her eyebrows. "Did you choose your own subject?"

"No; Miss Dearborn thought we were not old enough to find good ones."

"What were some of the others?"

" 'Fireside Reveries,' 'Grant as a Soldier,' 'Reflections on the Life of P. T. Barnum,' 'Buried Cities'; I can't remember any more now. They were all bad, and I can't bear to show them; I can write poetry easier and better, Miss Maxwell."

"Poetry!" she exclaimed. "Did Miss Dearborn require you to do it?"

"Oh, no; I always did it even at the farm. Shall I bring all I have? It isn't much."

Rebecca took the blank-book in which she kept copies of her effusions and left it at Miss Maxwell's door, hoping that she might be asked in and thus obtain a private interview; but a servant answered her ring, and she could only walk away, disappointed.

A few days afterward she saw the black-covered book on Miss Maxwell's desk and knew that the dreaded moment

of criticism had come, so she was not surprised to be asked
to remain after class.

The room was quiet; the red leaves rustled in the breeze
and flew in at the open window, bearing the first compliments of the season. Miss Maxwell came and sat by Rebecca's side on the bench.

"Did you think these were good?" she asked, giving her
the verses.

"Not so very," confessed Rebecca; "but it's hard to tell
all by yourself. The Perkinses and the Cobbs always said
they were wonderful, but when Mrs. Cobb told me she
thought they were better than Mr. Longfellow's I was worried, because I knew that couldn't be true."

This ingenuous remark confirmed Miss Maxwell's opinion
of Rebecca as a girl who could hear the truth and profit by
it.

"Well, my child," she said smilingly, "your friends were
wrong and you were right; judged by the proper tests, they
are pretty bad."

"Then I must give up all hope of ever being a writer!"
sighed Rebecca, who was tasting the bitterness of hemlock
and wondering if she could keep the tears back until the
interview was over.

"Don't go so fast," interrupted Miss Maxwell. "Though
they don't amount to anything as poetry, they show a good
deal of promise in certain directions. You almost never make
a mistake in rhyme or meter, and this shows you have
a natural sense of what is right; a 'sense of form,' poets
would call it. When you grow older, have a little more experience,—in fact, when you have something to say, I think

you may write very good verses. Poetry needs knowledge and vision, experience and imagination, Rebecca. You have not the first three yet, but I rather think you have a touch of the last."

"Must I never try any more poetry, not even to amuse myself?"

"Certainly you may; it will only help you to write better prose. Now for the first composition. I am going to ask all the new students to write a letter giving some description of the town and a hint of the school life."

"Shall I have to be myself?" asked Rebecca.

"What do you mean?"

"A letter from Rebecca Randall to her sister Hannah at Sunnybrook Farm, or to her Aunt Jane at the brick house, Riverboro, is so dull and stupid, if it is a real letter; but if I could make-believe I was a different girl altogether, and write to somebody who would be sure to understand everything I said, I could make it nicer."

"Very well; I think that's a delightful plan," said Miss Maxwell; "and who will you suppose yourself to be?"

"I like heiresses very much," replied Rebecca contemplatively. "Of course I never saw one, but interesting things are always happening to heiresses, especially to the golden-haired kind. My heiress wouldn't be vain and haughty like the wicked sisters in 'Cinderella'; she would be noble and generous. She would give up a grand school in Boston because she wanted to come here where her father lived when he was a boy, long before he made his fortune. The father is dead now, and she has a guardian, the best and kindest man in the world; he is rather old of course, and sometimes very

quiet and grave, but sometimes when he is happy, he is full of fun, and then Evelyn is not afraid of him. Yes, the girl shall be called Evelyn Abercrombie, and her guardian's name shall be Mr. Adam Ladd."

"Do you know Mr. Ladd?" asked Miss Maxwell in surprise.

"Yes, he's my very best friend," cried Rebecca delightedly. "Do you know him too?"

"Oh, yes; he is a trustee of these schools, you know, and often comes here. But if I let you 'suppose' any more, you will tell me your whole letter and then I shall lose a pleasant surprise."

What Rebecca thought of Miss Maxwell we already know; how the teacher regarded the pupil may be gathered from the following letter written two or three months later:—

WAREHAM, December 1st.

MY DEAR FATHER,—As you well know, I have-not always been an enthusiast on the subject of teaching. The task of cramming knowledge into these self-sufficient, inefficient youngsters of both sexes discourages me at times. The more stupid they are, the less they are aware of it. If my department were geography or mathematics, I believe I should feel that I was accomplishing something, for in those branches application and industry work wonders; but in English literature and composition one yearns for brains, for appreciation, for imagination! Month after month I toil on, opening oyster after oyster, but seldom finding a pearl. Fancy my joy this term when, without any violent effort at shell-splitting, I came upon a rare pearl; a black one, but of satin skin and beautiful luster! Her name is Rebecca, and she looks not unlike Rebekah at the Well in our family Bible; her hair and eyes being so dark as to suggest a strain of Italian or Spanish blood. She is nobody in particular. Man has done nothing for her; she has no family to speak of, no money, no education worthy the name, has had no advantages of any sort; but Dame Nature flung herself into the breach and said:—

> This child I to myself will take;
> She shall be mine and I will make
> A Lady of my own.

Blessed Wordsworth! How he makes us understand! And the pearl never heard of him until now! Think of reading Lucy to a class, and when you finish, seeing a fourteen-year-old pair of lips quivering with delight, and a pair of eyes brimming with comprehending tears!

You poor darling! You, too, know the discouragement of sowing lovely seed in rocky earth, in sand, in water, and (it almost seems sometimes) in mud; knowing that if anything comes up at all it will be some poor starveling plant. Fancy the joy of finding a real mind; of dropping seed in a soil so warm, so fertile, that one knows there are sure to be foliage, blossoms, and fruit all in good time! I wish I were not so impatient and so greedy of results! I am not fit to be a teacher; no one is who is so scornful of stupidity as I am. . . . The pearl writes quaint countrified little verses, doggerel they are; but somehow or other she always contrives to put in one line, one thought, one image, that shows you she is, quite unconsciously to herself, in possession of the secret. . . . Good-bye; I'll bring Rebecca home with me some Friday, and let you and mother see her for yourselves.

Your affectionate daughter,

EMILY.

Chapter Nineteen

Clover Blossoms and Sunflowers

How d' ye do, girls?" said Huldah Meserve, peeping in at the door. "Can you stop studying a minute and show me your room? Say, I've just been down to the store and bought me these gloves, for I was bound I wouldn't wear mittens this winter; they're simply too countrified. It's your first year here, and you're younger than I am, so I s'pose you don't mind, but I simply suffer if I don't keep up some kind of style. Say, your room is simply too cute for words! I don't believe any of the others can begin to compare with it! I don't know what gives it that simply gorgeous look, whether it's the full curtains, or that elegant screen, or Rebecca's lamp; but you certainly do have a faculty for fixing up. I like a pretty room too, but I never have a minute to attend to mine; I'm always so busy on my clothes that half the time I don't get my bed made up till noon; and after all, having no callers but the girls, it don't make much difference. When I graduate, I'm going to fix up our parlor at home so it'll be simply regal. I've learned decalcomania, and after I take up luster painting I shall have it simply stiff with drapes and tidies and plaques and sofa pillows, and make mother let me have a fire, and receive my friends there evenings. May I dry my feet at your register? I can't bear to wear rubbers unless the mud or the slush is simply knee-deep, they make your feet look so awfully big. I had such a fuss getting this pair of French-heeled boots that I don't intend to spoil the looks of them with rubbers any oftener than I can help. I believe boys notice feet quicker than anything. Elmer Webster stepped on one of mine yesterday when I accidentally had it out in the aisle, and when he apologized after class, he said he wasn't so much to blame, for the foot was so little he really couldn't see it! Isn't he perfectly great? Of course that's only his way of talking, for after all I only wear a number two, but these French heels and pointed toes do certainly make your foot look smaller, and it's always said a high instep helps, too. I used to think mine was almost a deformity, but they say it's a great beauty. Just put your feet beside mine, girls, and look at the difference; not that I care much, but just for fun."

"My feet are very comfortable where they are," responded Rebecca dryly. "I can't stop to measure insteps on algebra days; I've noticed your habit of keeping a foot in the aisle ever since you had those new shoes, so I don't wonder it was stepped on."

"Perhaps I am a little mite conscious of them, because they're not so very comfortable at first, till you get them broken in. Say, haven't you got a lot of new things?"

"Our Christmas presents, you mean," said Emma Jane.

"The pillow-cases are from Mrs. Cobb, the rug from cousin Mary in North Riverboro, the scrap-basket from Living and Dick. We gave each other the bureau and cushion covers, and the screen is mine from Mr. Ladd."

"Well, you were lucky when you met him! Gracious! I wish I could meet somebody like that. The way he keeps it up, too! It just hides your bed, doesn't it, and I always say that a bed takes the style off any room—specially when it's not made up; though you have an alcove, and it's the only one in the whole building. I don't see how you managed to get this good room when you're such new scholars," she finished discontentedly.

"We shouldn't have, except that Ruth Berry had to go away suddenly on account of her father's death. This room was empty, and Miss Maxwell asked if we might have it," returned Emma Jane.

"The great and only Max is more stiff and stand-offish than ever this year," said Huldah. "I've simply given up trying to please her, for there's no justice in her; she is good to her favorites, but she doesn't pay the least attention to anybody else, except to make sarcastic speeches about things that are none of her business. I wanted to tell her yesterday it was her place to teach me Latin, not manners."

"I wish you wouldn't talk against Miss Maxwell to me," said Rebecca hotly. "You know how I feel."

"I know; but I can't understand how you can abide her."

"I not only abide, I love her!" exclaimed Rebecca. "I wouldn't let the sun shine too hot on her, or the wind blow too cold. I'd like to put a marble platform in her class-room and have her sit in a velvet chair behind a golden table!"

"Well, don't have a fit!—because she can sit where she likes for all of me; I've got something better to think of." And Huldah tossed her head.

"Isn't this your study hour?" asked Emma Jane, to stop possible discussion.

"Yes, but I lost my Latin grammar yesterday; I left it in the hall half an hour while I was having a regular scene with Herbert Dunn. I haven't spoken to him for a week and gave him back his class pin. He was simply furious. Then when I came back to the hall, the book was gone. I had to go down town for my gloves and to the principal's office to see if the grammar had been handed in, and that's the reason I'm so fine."

Huldah was wearing a woolen dress that had once been gray, but had been dyed a brilliant blue. She had added three rows of white braid and large white pearl buttons to her gray jacket, in order to make it a little more "dressy." Her gray felt hat had a white feather on it, and a white tissue veil with large black dots made her delicate skin look brilliant. Rebecca thought how lovely the knot of red hair looked under the hat behind, and how the color of the front had been dulled by incessant frizzing with curling irons. Her open jacket disclosed a galaxy of souvenirs pinned to the background of bright blue,—a small American flag, a button of the Wareham Rowing Club, and one or two society pins. These decorations proved her popularity in very much the same way as do the cotillion favors hanging on the bedroom walls of the fashionable belle. She had been pinning and unpinning, arranging and disarranging her veil ever since she entered the room, in the hope that the girls would ask her whose ring she was wearing this week; but although both had noticed the new ornament instantly, wild horses could not have drawn the question from them; her desire to be asked was too obvious. With her gay plumage, her "nods and becks and wreathèd smiles," and her cheerful cackle, Huldah closely resembled the parrot in Wordsworth's poem:—

> Arch, volatile, a sportive bird,
>   By social glee inspired;
> Ambitious to be seen or heard,
>   And pleased to be admired!

"Mr. Morrison thinks the grammar will be returned, and lent me another," Huldah continued. "He was rather snippy about my leaving a book in the hall. There was a perfectly elegant gentleman in the office, a stranger to me. I wish he was a new teacher, but there's no such luck. He was too young to be the father of any of the girls, and too old to be a brother, but he was handsome as a picture and had on an awful stylish suit of clothes. He looked at me about every minute I was in the room. It made me so embarrassed I couldn't hardly answer Mr. Morrison's questions straight."

"You'll have to wear a mask pretty soon, if you're going to have any comfort, Huldah," said Rebecca. "Did he offer to lend you his class pin, or has it been so long since he graduated that he's left off wearing it? And tell us now whether the principal asked for a lock of your hair to put in his watch?"

This was all said merrily and laughingly, but there were times when Huldah could scarcely make up her mind whether Rebecca was trying to be witty, or whether she was jealous; but she generally decided it was merely the latter feeling, rather natural in a girl who had little attention.

"He wore no jewelry but a cameo scarf pin and a perfectly gorgeous ring,—a queer kind of one that wound round and round his finger. Oh, dear, I must run! Where has the hour gone? There's the study bell!"

Rebecca had pricked up her ears at Huldah's speech. She remembered a certain strange ring, and it belonged to the only person in the world (save Miss Maxwell) who appealed to her imagination,—Mr. Aladdin. Her feeling for him, and that of Emma Jane, was a mixture of romantic and reverent admiration for the man himself and the liveliest gratitude for his beautiful gifts. Since they first met him not a Christmas had gone by without some remembrance for them both; remembrances chosen with the rarest taste and forethought. Emma Jane had seen him only twice, but he had called several times at the brick house, and Rebecca had learned to know him better. It was she, too, who always wrote the notes of acknowledgment and thanks, taking infinite pains to make Emma Jane's quite different from her own. Sometimes he had written from Boston and asked her the news of Riverboro, and she had sent him pages of quaint and childlike gossip, interspersed, on two occasions, with poetry, which he read and reread with infinite relish. If Huldah's stranger should be Mr. Aladdin, would he come to see her, and could she and Emma Jane show him their beautiful room with so many of his gifts in evidence?

When the girls had established themselves in Wareham as real boarding pupils, it seemed to them existence was as full of joy as it well could hold. This first winter was, in

fact, the most tranquilly happy of Rebecca's school life,—a
winter long to be looked back upon. She and Emma Jane
were room-mates, and had put their modest possessions
together to make their surroundings pretty and homelike.
The room had, to begin with, a cheerful red ingrain carpet
and a set of maple furniture. As to the rest, Rebecca had
furnished the ideas and Emma Jane the materials and labor,
a method of dividing responsibilities that seemed to suit the
circumstances admirably. Mrs. Perkins's father had been a
storekeeper, and on his death had left the goods of which he
was possessed to his married daughter. The molasses, vine-
gar, and kerosene had lasted the family for five years, and
the Perkins attic was still a treasure-house of ginghams,
cottons, and "Yankee notions." So at Rebecca's instigation
Mrs. Perkins had made full curtains and lambrequins of unbleached muslin, which she had trimmed and looped back
with bands of Turkey red cotton. There were two table
covers to match, and each of the girls had her study corner.
Rebecca, after much coaxing, had been allowed to bring
over her precious lamp, which would have given a luxurious
air to any apartment, and when Mr. Aladdin's last Christmas presents were added,—the Japanese screen for Emma
Jane and the little shelf of English Poets for Rebecca,—they
declared that it was all quite as much fun as being married
and going to housekeeping.

The day of Huldah's call was Friday, and on Fridays from
three to half-past four Rebecca was free to take a pleasure
to which she looked forward the entire week. She always
ran down the snowy path through the pine woods at the
back of the seminary, and coming out on a quiet village
street, went directly to the large white house where Miss

Maxwell lived. The maid-of-all-work answered her knock; she took off her hat and cape and hung them in the hall, put her rubber shoes and umbrella carefully in the corner, and then opened the door of paradise. Miss Maxwell's sitting-room was lined on two sides with bookshelves, and Rebecca was allowed to sit before the fire and browse among the books to her heart's delight for an hour or more. Then Miss Maxwell would come back from her class, and there would be a precious half hour of chat before Rebecca had to meet Emma Jane at the station and take the train for Riverboro, where her Saturdays and Sundays were spent, and where she was washed, ironed, mended, and examined, approved and reproved, warned and advised in quite sufficient quantity to last her the succeeding week.

On this Friday she buried her face in the blooming geraniums on Miss Maxwell's plant-stand, selected "Romola" from one of the book-cases, and sank into a seat by the window with a sigh of infinite content. She glanced at the clock now and then, remembering the day on which she had been so immersed in "David Copperfield" that the Riverboro train had no place in her mind. The distracted Emma Jane had refused to leave without her, and had run from the station to look for her at Miss Maxwell's. There was but one later train, and that went only to a place three miles the other side of Riverboro, so that the two girls appeared at their respective homes long after dark, having had a weary walk in the snow.

When she had read for half an hour she glanced out of the window and saw two figures issuing from the path through the woods. The knot of bright hair and the coquettish hat could belong to but one person; and her companion,

as the couple approached, proved to be none other than Mr.
Aladdin. Huldah was lifting her skirts daintily and picking
safe stepping-places for the high-heeled shoes, her cheeks
glowing, her eyes sparkling under the black and white veil.

Rebecca slipped from her post by the window to the rug
before the bright fire and leaned her head on the seat of the
great easy-chair. She was frightened at the storm in her
heart; at the suddenness with which it had come on, as well
as at the strangeness of an entirely new sensation. She felt
all at once as if she could not bear to give up her share of Mr.
Aladdin's friendship to Huldah: Huldah so bright, saucy,
and pretty; so gay and ready, and such good company! She
had always joyfully admitted Emma Jane into the precious
partnership, but perhaps unconsciously to herself she had
realized that Emma Jane had never held anything but a
secondary place in Mr. Aladdin's regard; yet who was she
herself, after all, that she could hope to be first?

Suddenly the door opened softly and somebody looked
in, somebody who said: "Miss Maxwell told me I should find
Miss Rebecca Randall here."

Rebecca started at the sound and sprang to her feet, saying joyfully, "Mr. Aladdin! Oh! I knew you were in Wareham, and I was afraid you wouldn't have time to come and
see us."

"Who is 'us'? The aunts are not here, are they? Oh, you
mean the rich blacksmith's daughter, whose name I can
never remember. Is she here?"

"Yes, and my room-mate," answered Rebecca, who
thought her own knell of doom had sounded, if he had forgotten Emma Jane's name.

The light in the room grew softer, the fire crackled

cheerily, and they talked of many things, until the old sweet
sense of friendliness and familiarity crept back into Rebecca's heart. Adam had not seen her for several months,
and there was much to be learned about school matters as
viewed from her own standpoint; he had already inquired
concerning her progress from Mr. Morrison.

"Well, little Miss Rebecca," he said, rousing himself at
length, "I must be thinking of my drive to Portland. There
is a meeting of railway directors there to-morrow, and I always take this opportunity of visiting the school and giving
my valuable advice concerning its affairs, educational and
financial."

"It seems funny for you to be a school trustee," said Rebecca contemplatively. "I can't seem to make it fit."

"You are a remarkably wise young person and I quite
agree with you," he answered; "the fact is," he added
soberly, "I accepted the trusteeship in memory of my poor
little mother, whose last happy years were spent here."

"That was a long time ago!"

"Let me see, I am thirty-two; only thirty-two, despite an
occasional gray hair. My mother was married a month after
she graduated, and she lived only until I was ten; yes, it is a
long way back to my mother's time here, though the school
was fifteen or twenty years old then, I believe. Would you
like to see my mother, Miss Rebecca?"

The girl took the leather case gently and opened it to find
an innocent, pink-and-white daisy of a face, so confiding,
so sensitive, that it went straight to the heart. It made Rebecca feel old, experienced, and maternal. She longed on
the instant to comfort and strengthen such a tender young
thing.

"Oh, what a sweet, sweet, flowery face!" she whispered softly.

"The flower had to bear all sorts of storms," said Adam gravely. "The bitter weather of the world bent its slender stalk, bowed its head, and dragged it to the earth. I was only a child and could do nothing to protect and nourish it, and there was no one else to stand between it and trouble. Now I have success and money and power, all that would have kept her alive and happy, and it is too late. She died for lack of love and care, nursing and cherishing, and I can never forget it. All that has come to me seems now and then so useless, since I cannot share it with her!"

This was a new Mr. Aladdin, and Rebecca's heart gave a throb of sympathy and comprehension. This explained the tired look in his eyes, the look that peeped out now and then, under all his gay speech and laughter.

"I'm so glad I know," she said, "and so glad I could see her just as she was when she tied that white muslin hat under her chin and saw her yellow curls and her sky-blue eyes in the glass. Mustn't she have been happy! I wish she could have been kept so, and have lived to see you grow up strong and good. My mother is always sad and busy, but once when she looked at John I heard her say, 'He makes up for everything.' That's what your mother would have thought about you if she had lived—and perhaps she does as it is."

"You are a comforting little person, Rebecca," said Adam, rising from his chair.

As Rebecca rose, the tears still trembling on her lashes, he looked at her suddenly as with new vision.

"Good-bye!" he said, taking her slim brown hands in his,

adding, as if he saw her for the first time, "Why, little Rose-Red-Snow-White is making way for a new girl! Burning the midnight oil and doing four years' work in three is supposed to dull the eye and blanch the cheek, yet Rebecca's eyes are bright and she has a rosy color! Her long braids are looped one on the other so that they make a black letter U behind, and they are tied with grand bows at the top! She is so tall that she reaches almost to my shoulder. This will never do in the world! How will Mr. Aladdin get on without his comforting little friend! He doesn't like grown-up young ladies in wonderful fine clothes; they frighten and bore him!"

"Oh, Mr. Aladdin!" cried Rebecca eagerly, taking his jest quite seriously; "I am not fifteen yet, and it will be three years before I'm a young lady; please don't give me up until you have to!"

"I won't; I promise you that," said Adam. "Rebecca," he continued, after a moment's pause, "who is that young girl with a lot of pretty red hair and very citified manners? She escorted me down the hill; do you know whom I mean?"

"It must be Huldah Meserve; she is from Riverboro."

Adam put a finger under Rebecca's chin and looked into her eyes; eyes as soft, as clear, as unconscious, and childlike as they had been when she was ten. He remembered the other pair of challenging blue ones that had darted coquettish glances through half-dropped lids, shot arrowy beams from under archly lifted brows, and said gravely, "Don't form yourself on her, Rebecca; clover blossoms that grow in the fields beside Sunnybrook mustn't be tied in the same bouquet with gaudy sunflowers; they are too sweet and fragrant and wholesome."

Chapter Twenty

The Hill Difficulty

The first happy year at Wareham, with its widened sky-line, its larger vision, its greater opportunity, was over and gone. Rebecca had studied during the summer vacation, and had passed, on her return in the autumn, certain examinations which would enable her, if she carried out the same programme the next season, to complete the course in three instead of four years. She came off with no flying colors,—that would have been impossible in consideration of her inadequate training; but she did wonderfully well in some of the required subjects, and so brilliantly in others that the average was respectable. She would never have been a remarkable scholar under any circumstances, perhaps, and she was easily outstripped in mathematics and the natural sciences by a dozen girls, but in some inexplicable way she became, as the months went on, the foremost figure in the school. When she had entirely forgotten the facts which would enable her to answer a question fully and conclusively, she commonly had some original theory to expound; it was not always correct, but it was generally unique and sometimes amusing. She was only fair in Latin or French grammar, but when it came to translation, her freedom, her choice of words, and her sympathetic understanding of the spirit of the text made her the delight of her teachers and the despair of her rivals.

"She can be perfectly ignorant of a subject," said Miss Maxwell to Adam Ladd, "but entirely intelligent the moment she has a clue. Most of the other girls are full of information and as stupid as sheep."

Rebecca's gifts had not been discovered save by the few, during the first year, when she was adjusting herself quietly to the situation. She was distinctly one of the poorer girls; she had no fine dresses to attract attention, no visitors, no friends in the town. She had more study hours, and less time, therefore, for the companionship of other girls, gladly as she would have welcomed the gayety of that side of school life. Still, water will find its own level in some way, and by the spring of the second year she had naturally settled into the same sort of leadership which had been hers in the smaller community of Riverboro. She was unanimously elected assistant editor of the Wareham School "Pilot," being the first girl to assume that enviable, though somewhat arduous and thankless position, and when her maiden number went to the Cobbs, Uncle Jerry and Aunt Sarah could hardly eat or sleep for pride.

"She'll always get votes," said Huldah Meserve, when discussing the election, "for whether she knows anything or not, she looks as if she did, and whether she's capable of filling an office or not, she looks as if she was. I only wish I was tall and dark and had the gift of making people believe I was great things, like Rebecca Randall. There's one thing: though the boys call her handsome, you notice they don't trouble her with much attention."

It was a fact that Rebecca's attitude towards the opposite sex was still somewhat indifferent and oblivious, even for fifteen and a half! No one could look at her and doubt that she had potentialities of attraction latent within her somewhere, but that side of her nature was happily biding its time. A human being is capable only of a certain amount of activity at a given moment, and it will inevitably satisfy first its most pressing needs, its most ardent desires, its chief ambitions. Rebecca was full of small anxieties and fears, for matters were not going well at the brick house, and were anything but hopeful at the home farm. She was overbusy and overtaxed, and her thoughts were naturally drawn towards the difficult problems of daily living.

It had seemed to her during the autumn and winter of that year as if her Aunt Miranda had never been, save at the very first, so censorious and so fault-finding. One Saturday Rebecca ran upstairs and, bursting into a flood of tears, exclaimed, "Aunt Jane, it seems as if I never could stand her continual scoldings. Nothing I can do suits Aunt Miranda; she's just said it will take me my whole life to get the Randall out of me, and I'm not convinced that I want it all out, so there we are!"

Aunt Jane, never demonstrative, cried with Rebecca as she attempted to soothe her.

"You must be patient," she said, wiping first her own eyes and then Rebecca's. "I haven't told you, for it isn't fair you should be troubled when you're studying so hard, but your

Aunt Miranda isn't well. One Monday morning about a month ago, she had a kind of faint spell; it wasn't bad but the doctor is afraid it was a shock, and if so, it's the beginning of the end. Seems to me she's failing right along, and that's what makes her so fretful and easy vexed. She has other troubles too, that you don't know anything about, and if you're not kind to your Aunt Miranda now, child, you'll be dreadful sorry some time."

All the temper faded from Rebecca's face, and she stopped crying to say penitently, "Oh! the poor dear thing! I won't mind a bit what she says now. She's just asked me for some milk toast and I was dreading to take it to her, but this will make everything different. Don't worry yet, Aunt Jane, for perhaps it won't be as bad as you think."

So when she carried the toast to her aunt a little later, it was in the best gilt-edged china bowl, with a fringed napkin on the tray and a sprig of geranium lying across the salt-cellar.

"Now, Aunt Miranda," she said cheerily, "I expect you to smack your lips and say this is good; it's not Randall, but Sawyer milk toast."

"You've tried all kinds on me, one time an' another," Miranda answered. "This tastes real kind o' good; but I wish you hadn't wasted that nice geranium."

"You can't tell what's wasted," said Rebecca philosophically; "perhaps that geranium has been hoping this long time it could brighten somebody's supper, so don't disappoint it by making believe you don't like it. I've seen geraniums cry,—in the very early morning!"

The mysterious trouble to which Jane had alluded was a

very real one, but it was held in profound secrecy. Twenty-
five hundred dollars of the small Sawyer property had been
invested in the business of a friend of their father's, and had
returned them a regular annual income of a hundred dollars. The family friend had been dead for some five years,
but his son had succeeded to his interests and all went on as
formerly. Suddenly there came a letter saying that the firm
had gone into bankruptcy, that the business had been com-
pletely wrecked, and that the Sawyer money had been swept
away with everything else.

The loss of one hundred dollars a year is a very trifling matter, but it made all the difference between comfort and self-
denial to the two old spinsters. Their manner of life had
been so rigid and careful that it was difficult to economize
any further, and the blow had fallen just when it was most
inconvenient, for Rebecca's school and boarding expenses,
small as they were, had to be paid promptly and in cash.

"Can we possibly go on doing it? Shan't we have to give
up and tell her why?" asked Jane tearfully to the elder sister.

"We have put our hand to the plough, and we can't turn
back," answered Miranda in her grimmest tone; "we've
taken her away from her mother and offered her an education, and we've got to keep our word. She's Aurelia's only
hope for years to come, to my way o' thinkin'. Hannah's
beau takes all her time 'n' thought, and when she gits a husband her mother'll be out o' sight and out o' mind. John,
instead of farmin', thinks he must be a doctor,—as if folks
wasn't gettin' unhealthy enough these days, without turnin'
out more young doctors to help 'em into their graves. No,
Jane; we'll skimp 'n' do without, 'n' plan to git along on our

interest money somehow, but we won't break into our principal, whatever happens."

"Breaking into the principal" was, in the minds of most thrifty New England women, a sin only second to arson, theft, or murder; and, though the rule was occasionally carried too far for common sense,—as in this case, where two elderly women of sixty might reasonably have drawn something from their little hoard in time of special need,—it doubtless wrought more of good than evil in the community.

Rebecca, who knew nothing of their business affairs, merely saw her aunts grow more and more saving, pinching here and there, cutting off this and that relentlessly. Less meat and fish were bought; the woman who had lately been coming two days a week for washing, ironing, and scrubbing was dismissed; the old bonnets of the season before were brushed up and retrimmed; there were no drives to Moderation or trips to Portland. Economy was carried to its very extreme; but though Miranda was well-nigh as gloomy and uncompromising in her manner and conversation as a woman could well be, she at least never twitted her niece of being a burden; so Rebecca's share of the Sawyers' misfortunes consisted only in wearing her old dresses, hats, and jackets, without any apparent hope of a change.

There was, however, no concealing the state of things at Sunnybrook, where chapters of accidents had unfolded themselves in a sort of serial story that had run through the year. The potato crop had failed; there were no apples to speak of; the hay had been poor; Aurelia had turns of dizziness in her head; Mark had broken his ankle. As this was his fourth offense, Miranda inquired how many bones there were in the human body, "so 't they'd know when Mark got through breakin' 'em." The time for paying the interest on the mortgage, that incubus that had crushed all the joy out of the Randall household, had come and gone, and there was no possibility, for the first time in fourteen years, of paying the required forty-eight dollars. The only bright spot in the horizon was Hannah's engagement to Will Melville,— a young farmer whose land joined Sunnybrook, who had a good house, was alone in the world, and his own master. Hannah was so satisfied with her own unexpectedly radiant prospects that she hardly realized her mother's anxieties; for there are natures which flourish in adversity, and deteriorate when exposed to sudden prosperity. She had made a visit of a week at the brick house; and Miranda's impression, conveyed in privacy to Jane, was that Hannah was close as the bark of a tree, and consid'able selfish too; that when she'd clim' as fur as she could in the world, she'd kick the ladder out from under her, everlastin' quick; that, on being sounded as to her ability to be of use to the younger children in the future, she said she guessed she'd done her share a'ready, and she wa'n't goin' to burden Will with her poor relations. "She's Susan Randall through and through!" ejaculated Miranda. "I was glad to see her face turned towards Temperance. If that mortgage is ever cleared from the farm, 't won't be Hannah that'll do it; it'll be Rebecca or me!"

Chapter Twenty-One

Aladdin Rubs His Lamp

Your esteemed contribution entitled 'Wareham Wild-flowers' has been accepted for 'The Pilot,' Miss Perkins," said Rebecca, entering the room where Emma Jane was darning the firm's stockings. "I stayed to tea with Miss Maxwell, but came home early to tell you."

"You are joking, Becky!" faltered Emma Jane, looking up from her work.

"Not a bit; the senior editor read it and thought it highly instructive; it appears in the next issue."

"Not in the same number with your poem about the golden gates that close behind us when we leave school?" And Emma Jane held her breath as she awaited the reply.

"Even so, Miss Perkins."

"Rebecca," said Emma Jane, with the nearest approach to tragedy that her nature would permit, "I don't know as I shall be able to bear it, and if anything happens to me, I ask you solemnly to bury that number of 'The Pilot' with me."

Rebecca did not seem to think this the expression of an exaggerated state of feeling, inasmuch as she replied, "I

199

know; that's just the way it seemed to me at first, and even now, whenever I'm alone and take out the 'Pilot' back numbers to read over my contributions, I almost burst with pleasure; and it's not that they are good either, for they look worse to me every time I read them."

"If you would only live with me in some little house when we get older," mused Emma Jane, as with her darning needle poised in air she regarded the opposite wall dreamily, "I would do the housework and cooking, and copy all your poems and stories, and take them to the post-office, and you needn't do anything but write. It would be perfectly elergant!"

"I'd like nothing better, if I hadn't promised to keep house for John," replied Rebecca.

"He won't have a house for a good many years, will he?"

"No," sighed Rebecca ruefully, flinging herself down by the table and resting her head on her hand. "Not unless we can contrive to pay off that detestable mortgage. The day grows farther off instead of nearer now that we haven't paid the interest this year."

She pulled a piece of paper towards her, and scribbling idly on it read aloud in a moment or two:—

"Will you pay a little faster?" said the mortgage to the farm;
    "I confess I'm very tired of this place."
"The weariness is mutual," Rebecca Randall cried;
    "I would I'd never gazed upon your face!"

"A note has a 'face,'" observed Emma Jane, who was gifted in arithmetic. "I didn't know that a mortgage had."

"Our mortgage has," said Rebecca revengefully. "I should know him if I met him in the dark. Wait and I'll draw him for you. It will be good for you to know how he looks, and then when you have a husband and seven children, you won't allow him to come anywhere within a mile of your farm."

The sketch when completed was of a sort to be shunned by a timid person on the verge of slumber. There was a tiny house on the right, and a weeping family gathered in front of it. The mortgage was depicted as a cross between a fiend and an ogre, and held an axe uplifted in his red right hand. A figure with streaming black locks was staying the blow, and this, Rebecca explained complacently, was intended as a likeness of herself, though she was rather vague as to the method she should use in attaining her end.

"He's terrible," said Emma Jane, "but awfully wizened and small."

"It's only a twelve-hundred-dollar mortgage," said Rebecca, "and that's called a small one. John saw a man once that was mortgaged for twelve thousand."

"Shall you be a writer or an editor?" asked Emma Jane presently, as if one had only to choose and the thing were done.

"I shall have to do what turns up first, I suppose."

"Why not go out as a missionary to Syria, as the Burches are always coaxing you to? The Board would pay your expenses."

"I can't make up my mind to be a missionary," Rebecca answered. "I'm not good enough in the first place, and I don't 'feel a call,' as Mr. Burch says you must. I would like to do something for somebody and make things move, somewhere, but I don't want to go thousands of miles away teaching people how to live when I haven't learned myself. It isn't as if the heathen really needed me; I'm sure they'll come out all right in the end."

"I can't see how; if all the people who ought to go out to save them stay at home as we do," argued Emma Jane.

"Why, whatever God is, and wherever He is, He must always be there, ready and waiting. He can't move about and miss people. It may take the heathen a little longer to find Him, but God will make allowances, of course. He knows if they live in such hot climates it must make them lazy and slow; and the parrots and tigers and snakes and bread-fruit trees distract their minds; and having no books, they can't think as well; but they'll find God somehow, some time."

"What if they die first?" asked Emma Jane.

"Oh, well, they can't be blamed for that; they don't die on purpose," said Rebecca, with a comfortable theology.

In these days Adam Ladd sometimes went to Temperance on business connected with the proposed branch of the railroad familiarly known as the "York and Yank'em," and while there he gained an inkling of Sunnybrook affairs. The building of the new road was not yet a certainty, and there was a difference of opinion as to the best route from Temperance to Plumville. In one event the way would lead directly through Sunnybrook, from corner to corner, and Mrs. Randall would be compensated; in the other, her interests would not be affected, either for good or ill, save as all land in the immediate neighborhood might rise a little in value.

Coming from Temperance to Wareham one day, Adam had a long walk and talk with Rebecca, whom he thought looking pale and thin, though she was holding bravely to her self-imposed hours of work. She was wearing a black cashmere dress that had been her Aunt Jane's second best. We are familiar with the heroine of romance whose foot is so exquisitely shaped that the coarsest shoe cannot conceal its perfections, and one always cherishes a doubt of the statement; yet it is true that Rebecca's peculiar and individual charm seemed wholly independent of accessories. The lines of her figure, the rare coloring of skin and hair and eyes, triumphed over shabby clothing, though, had the advantage of artistic apparel been given her, the little world of Wareham would probably at once have dubbed her a beauty. The long black braids were now disposed after a quaint fashion of her own. They were crossed behind, carried up to the front, and crossed again, the tapering ends finally brought down and hidden in the thicker part at the neck. Then a purely feminine touch was given to the hair that waved back from the face,—a touch that rescued little crests and wavelets from bondage and set them free to take a new color in the sun.

Adam Ladd looked at her in a way that made her put her hands over her face and laugh through them shyly as she said: "I know what you are thinking, Mr. Aladdin,—that my dress is an inch longer than last year, and my hair different; but I'm not nearly a young lady yet; truly I'm not. Sixteen is a month off still, and you promised not to give me up till my dress trails. If you don't like me to grow old, why don't you grow young? Then we can meet in the halfway house and have nice times. Now that I think about it," she continued, "that's just what you've been doing all along.

When you bought the soap, I thought you were Grandfather Sawyer's age; when you danced with me at the flag-raising, you seemed like my father; but when you showed me your mother's picture, I felt as if you were my John, because I was so sorry for you."

"That will do very well," smiled Adam; "unless you go so swiftly that you become my grandmother before I really need one. You are studying too hard, Miss Rebecca Rowena!"

"Just a little," she confessed. "But vacation comes soon, you know."

"And are you going to have a good rest and try to recover your dimples? They are really worth preserving."

A shadow crept over Rebecca's face and her eyes suffused. "Don't be kind, Mr. Aladdin, I can't bear it;—it's—it's not one of my dimply days!" And she ran in at the seminary gate, and disappeared with a farewell wave of her hand.

Adam Ladd wended his way to the principal's office in a thoughtful mood. He had come to Wareham to unfold a plan that he had been considering for several days. This year was the fiftieth anniversary of the founding of the Wareham schools, and he meant to tell Mr. Morrison that in addition to his gift of a hundred volumes to the reference library, he intended to celebrate it by offering prizes in English composition, a subject in which he was much interested. He wished the boys and girls of the two upper classes to compete, the award to be made to the writers of the two best essays. As to the nature of the prizes he had not quite made up his mind, but they would be substantial ones, either of money or of books.

This interview accomplished, he called upon Miss Maxwell, thinking as he took the path through the woods, "Rose-Red-Snow-White needs the help, and since there is no way of my giving it to her without causing remark, she must earn it, poor little soul! I wonder if my money is always to be useless where most I wish to spend it!"

He had scarcely greeted his hostess when he said: "Miss Maxwell, doesn't it strike you that our friend Rebecca looks wretchedly tired?"

"She does indeed, and I am considering whether I can take her away with me. I always go South for the spring vacation, traveling by sea to Old Point Comfort, and rusticating in some quiet spot near by. I should like nothing better than to have Rebecca for a companion."

"The very thing!" assented Adam heartily; "but why should you take the whole responsibility? Why not let me help? I am greatly interested in the child, and have been for some years."

"You needn't pretend you discovered her," interrupted Miss Maxwell warmly, "for I did that myself."

"She was an intimate friend of mine long before you ever came to Wareham," laughed Adam, and he told Miss Maxwell the circumstances of his first meeting with Rebecca. "From the beginning I've tried to think of a way I could be useful in her development, but no reasonable solution seemed to offer itself."

"Luckily she attends to her own development," answered Miss Maxwell. "In a sense she is independent of everything and everybody; she follows her saint without being conscious of it. But she needs a hundred practical things that money would buy for her, and alas! I have a slender purse."

"Take mine, I beg, and let me act through you," pleaded Adam. "I could not bear to see even a young tree trying its best to grow without light or air,—how much less a gifted child! I interviewed her aunts a year ago, hoping I might be permitted to give her a musical education. I assured them it was a most ordinary occurrence, and that I was willing to be repaid later on if they insisted, but it was no use. The elder Miss Sawyer remarked that no member of her family ever had lived on charity, and she guessed they wouldn't begin at this late day."

"I rather like that uncompromising New England grit," exclaimed Miss Maxwell, "and so far, I don't regret one burden that Rebecca has borne or one sorrow that she has shared. Necessity has only made her brave; poverty has only made her daring and self-reliant. As to her present needs, there are certain things only a woman ought to do for a girl, and I should not like to have you do them for Rebecca; I should feel that I was wounding her pride and self-respect, even though she were ignorant; but there is no reason why I may not do them if necessary and let you pay her traveling expenses. I would accept those for her without the slightest embarrassment, but I agree that the matter would better be kept private between us."

"You are a real fairy godmother!" exclaimed Adam, shaking her hand warmly. "Would it be less trouble for you to invite her room-mate too,—the pink-and-white inseparable?"

"No, thank you, I prefer to have Rebecca all to myself," said Miss Maxwell.

"I can understand that," replied Adam absent-mindedly; "I mean, of course, that one child is less trouble than two. There she is now."

Here Rebecca appeared in sight, walking down the quiet street with a lad of sixteen. They were in animated conversation, and were apparently reading something aloud to each other, for the black head and the curly brown one were both bent over a sheet of letter paper. Rebecca kept glancing up at her companion, her eyes sparkling with appreciation.

"Miss Maxwell," said Adam, "I am a trustee of this institution, but upon my word I don't believe in coeducation!"

"I have my own occasional hours of doubt," she answered, "but surely its disadvantages are reduced to a minimum with—children! That is a very impressive sight which you are privileged to witness, Mr. Ladd. The folk in Cambridge often gloated on the spectacle of Longfellow and Lowell arm in arm. The little school world of Wareham palpitates with excitement when it sees the senior and the junior editors of 'The Pilot' walking together!"

Chapter Twenty-Two

"Over the Teacups"

The summer term at Wareham had ended, and Huldah Meserve, Dick Carter, and Living Perkins had finished school, leaving Rebecca and Emma Jane to represent Riverboro in the year to come. Delia Weeks was at home from Lewiston on a brief visit, and Mrs. Robinson was celebrating the occasion by a small and select party, the particular day having been set because strawberries were ripe and there was a rooster that wanted killing. Mrs. Robinson explained this to her husband, and requested that he eat his dinner on the carpenter's bench in the shed, as the party was to be a ladies' affair.

"All right; it won't be any loss to me," said Mr. Robinson. "Give me beans, that's all I ask. When a rooster wants to be killed, I want somebody else to eat him, not me!"

Mrs. Robinson had company only once or twice a year, and was generally much prostrated for several days afterward, the struggle between pride and parsimony being quite too great a strain upon her. It was necessary, in order to maintain her standing in the community, to furnish a good "set out," yet the extravagance of the proceeding goaded her from the first moment she began to stir the marble cake to the moment when the feast appeared upon the table.

The rooster had been boiling steadily over a slow fire since morning, but such was his power of resistance that his shape was as firm and handsome in the pot as on the first moment when he was lowered into it.

"He ain't goin' to give up!" said Alice, peering nervously under the cover, "and he looks like a scarecrow."

"We'll see whether he gives up or not when I take a sharp knife to him," her mother answered; "and as to his looks, a platter full o' gravy makes a sight o' difference with old roosters, and I'll put dumplings round the aidge; they're turrible fillin', though they don't belong with boiled chicken."

The rooster did indeed make an impressive showing, lying in his border of dumplings, and the dish was much complimented when it was borne in by Alice. This was fortunate, as the chorus of admiration ceased abruptly when the ladies began to eat the fowl.

"I was glad you could git over to Huldy's graduation, Delia," said Mrs. Meserve, who sat at the foot of the table and helped the chicken while Mrs. Robinson poured coffee at the other end. She was a fit mother for Huldah, being much the most stylish person in Riverboro; ill health and dress were, indeed, her two chief enjoyments in life.

"How'd you like Huldy's dress, Delia?" she asked, snapping the elastic in her black jet bracelets after an irritating fashion she had.

"I thought it was about the handsomest of any," answered

Delia; "and her composition was first rate. It was the only real amusin' one there was, and she read it so loud and clear we didn't miss any of it; most o' the girls spoke as if they had hasty puddin' in their mouths."

"That was the composition she wrote for Adam Ladd's prize," explained Mrs. Meserve, "and they do say she'd 'a' come out first, 'stead o' fourth, if her subject had been dif'rent. There was three ministers and three deacons on the committee, and it was only natural they should choose a serious piece; hers was too lively to suit 'em."

Huldah's inspiring theme had been "Boys," and she certainly had a fund of knowledge and experience that fitted her to write most intelligently upon it. It was vastly popular with the audience, who enjoyed the rather cheap jokes and allusions with which it coruscated; but judged from a purely literary standpoint, it left much to be desired.

"Rebecca's piece wa'n't read out loud, but the one that took the boy's prize was; why was that?" asked Mrs. Robinson.

"Because she wa'n't graduatin'," explained Mrs. Cobb, "and couldn't take part in the exercises; it'll be printed, with Herbert Dunn's, in the school paper."

"I'm glad o' that, for I'll never believe it was better'n Huldy's till I read it with my own eyes; it seems as if the prize ought to 'a' gone to one of the seniors."

"Well, no, Marthy, not if Ladd offered it to any of the two upper classes that wanted to try for it," argued Mrs. Robinson. "They say they asked him to give out the prizes, and he refused, up and down. It seems odd, his bein' so rich and travelin' about all over the country, that he was too modest to git up on that platform."

"My Huldy could 'a' done it, and not winked an eyelash," observed Mrs. Meserve complacently; a remark which there seemed no disposition on the part of any of the company to controvert.

"It was complete, though, the governor happening to be there to see his niece graduate," said Delia Weeks. "Land! he looked elegant! They say he's only six feet, but he might 'a' been sixteen, and he certainly did make a fine speech."

"Did you notice Rebecca, how white she was, and how she trembled when she and Herbert Dunn stood there while the governor was praisin' 'em? He'd read her composition, too, for he wrote the Sawyer girls a letter about it." This remark was from the sympathetic Mrs. Cobb.

"I thought 't was kind o' foolish, his makin' so much of her when it wa'n't her graduation," objected Mrs. Meserve; "layin' his hand on her head 'n' all that, as if he was a Pope pronouncin' benediction. But there! I'm glad the prize come to Riverboro 't any rate, and a han'somer one never was give out from the Wareham platform. I guess there ain't no end to Adam Ladd's money. The fifty dollars would 'a' been good enough, but he must needs go and put it into those elegant purses."

"I set so fur back I couldn't see 'em fairly," complained Delia, "and now Rebecca has taken hers home to show her mother."

"It was kind of a gold net bag with a chain," said Mrs. Perkins, "and there was five ten-dollar gold pieces in it. Herbert Dunn's was put in a fine leather wallet."

"How long is Rebecca goin' to stay at the farm?" asked Delia.

"Till they get over Hannah's bein' married, and get the house to runnin' without her," answered Mrs. Perkins. "It seems as if Hannah might 'a' waited a little longer. Aurelia was set against her goin' away while Rebecca was at school, but she's obstinate as a mule, Hannah is, and she just took her own way in spite of her mother. She's been doin' her sewin' for a year; the awfulest coarse cotton cloth she had, but she's nearly blinded herself with fine stitchin' and rufflin' and tuckin'. Did you hear about the quilt she made?"

"She'd better 'a' been takin' in sewin' and earnin' money, 'stead o' blindin' her eyes on such foolishness as quilted counterpanes," said Mrs. Cobb. "The next thing you know that mortgage will be foreclosed on Mis' Randall, and she and the children won't have a roof over their heads."

"Don't they say there's a good chance of the railroad goin' through her place?" asked Mrs. Robinson. "If it does, she'll git as much as the farm is worth and more. Adam Ladd's one of the stockholders, and everything is a success he takes holt of. They're fightin' it in Augusty, but I'd back Ladd agin any o' them legislaters if he thought he was in the right."

"Rebecca'll have some new clothes now," said Delia, "and the land knows she needs 'em. Seems to me the Sawyer girls are gittin' turrible near!"

"Rebecca won't have any new clothes out o' the prize money," remarked Mrs. Perkins, "for she sent it away the next day to pay the interest on that mortgage."

"Poor little girl!" exclaimed Delia Weeks.

"She might as well help along her folks as spend it on foolishness," affirmed Mrs. Robinson. "I think she was mighty lucky to git it to pay the interest with, but she's probably like all the Randalls; it was easy come, easy go, with them."

"That's more than can be said of the Sawyer stock," retorted Mrs. Perkins; "seems like they enjoyed savin' more'n anything in the world, and it's gainin' on Mirandy sence her shock."

"I don't believe it was a shock; it stands to reason she'd never 'a' got up after it and been so smart as she is now; we had three o' the worst shocks in our family that there ever was on this river, and I know every symptom of 'em better'n the doctors." And Mrs. Peter Meserve shook her head wisely.

"Mirandy's smart enough," said Mrs. Cobb, "but you notice she stays right to home, and she's more close-mouthed than ever she was; never took a mite o' pride in the prize, as I could see, though it pretty nigh drove Jeremiah out o' his senses. I thought I should 'a' died o' shame when he cried 'Hooray!' and swung his straw hat when the governor shook hands with Rebecca. It's lucky he couldn't get fur into the church and had to stand back by the door, for as it was, he made a spectacle of himself. My suspicion is"— and here every lady stopped eating and sat up straight— "that the Sawyer girls have lost money. They don't know a thing about business 'n' never did, and Mirandy's too secretive and contrairy to ask advice."

"The most o' what they've got is in gov'ment bonds, I always heard, and you can't lose money on them. Jane had

the timber land left her, an' Mirandy had the brick house.
She probably took it awful hard that Rebecca's fifty dollars
had to be swallowed up in a mortgage, 'stead of goin' towards school expenses. The more I think of it, the more I
think Adam Ladd intended Rebecca should have that prize
when he gave it." The mind of Huldah's mother ran towards
the idea that her daughter's rights had been assailed.

"Land, Marthy, what foolishness you talk!" exclaimed
Mrs. Perkins; "you don't suppose he could tell what composition the committee was going to choose; and why should
he offer another fifty dollars for a boy's prize, if he wa'n't
interested in helpin' along the school? He's give Emma
Jane about the same present as Rebecca every Christmas
for five years; that's the way he does."

"Some time he'll forget one of 'em and give to the other, or
drop 'em both and give to some new girl!" said Delia Weeks,
with an experience born of fifty years of spinsterhood.

"Like as not," assented Mrs. Peter Meserve, "though it's
easy to see he ain't the marryin' kind. There's men that
would marry once a year if their wives would die fast
enough, and there's men that seems to want to live alone."

"If Ladd was a Mormon, I guess he could have every
woman in North Riverboro that's a suitable age, accordin'
to what my cousins say," remarked Mrs. Perkins.

"'Tain't likely he could be ketched by any North Riverboro girl," demurred Mrs. Robinson; "not when he prob-
'bly has had the pick o' Boston. I guess Marthy hit it when
she said there's men that ain't the marryin' kind."

"I wouldn't trust any of 'em when Miss Right comes
along!" laughed Mrs. Cobb genially. "You never can tell

what 'n' who's goin' to please 'em. You know Jeremiah's contrairy horse, Buster? He won't let anybody put the bit into
his mouth if he can help it. He'll fight Jerry, and fight me,
till he has to give in. Rebecca didn't know nothin' about
his tricks, and the other day she went int' the barn to hitch
up. I followed right along, knowing she'd have trouble with
the headstall, and I declare if she wa'n't pattin' Buster's
nose and talkin' to him, and when she put her little fingers
into his mouth he opened it so fur I thought he'd swaller her,
for sure. He jest smacked his lips over the bit as if 't was a
lump o' sugar. 'Land, Rebecca,' I says, 'how'd you persuade
him to take the bit?' 'I didn't,' she says, 'he seemed to want
it; perhaps he's tired of his stall and wants to get out in the
fresh air.'"

Chapter Twenty-Three

"*The Vision Splendid*"

A year had elapsed since Adam Ladd's prize had been discussed over the teacups in Riverboro. The months had come and gone, and at length the great day had dawned for Rebecca,—the day to which she had been looking forward for five years, as the first goal to be reached on her little journey through the world. School-days were ended, and the mystic function known to the initiated as "graduation" was about to be celebrated; it was even now heralded by the sun dawning in the eastern sky. Rebecca stole softly out of bed, crept to the window, threw open the blinds, and welcomed the rosy light that meant a cloudless morning. Even the sun looked different somehow,—larger, redder, more important than usual; and if it were really so, there was no member of the graduating class who would have thought it strange or unbecoming, in view of all the circumstances. Emma Jane stirred on her pillow, woke, and seeing Rebecca at the window, came and knelt on the floor beside her. "It's going to be pleasant!" she sighed gratefully. "If it wasn't wicked, I could thank the Lord, I'm so relieved in mind! Did you sleep?"

"Not much; the words of my class poem kept running through my head, and the accompaniments of the songs; and worse than anything, Mary Queen of Scots' prayer in Latin; it seemed as if

> "Adoro, imploro,
> Ut liberes me!

were burned into my brain."

No one who is unfamiliar with life in rural neighborhoods can imagine the gravity, the importance, the solemnity of this last day of school. In the matter of preparation, wealth of detail, and general excitement, it far surpasses a wedding. Wareham, then, was shaken to its very center on this day of days. Mothers and fathers of the scholars, as well as relatives to the remotest generation, had been coming on the train and driving into the town since breakfast time; old pupils, both married and single, with and without families, streamed back to the dear old village. The two livery stables were crowded with vehicles of all sorts, and lines of buggies and wagons were drawn up along the sides of the shady roads, the horses switching their tails in luxurious idleness. The streets were filled with people wearing their best clothes, and the fashions included not only "the latest thing," but the well-preserved relic of a bygone day. In the seminary building there was an excitement so deep and profound that it expressed itself in a kind of hushed silence, a transient suspension of life, as those most interested approached the crucial moment. The feminine graduates-to-be were seated in their own bedrooms, dressed with a completeness of detail to which all their past lives seemed to have been but a prelude. At least, this was the case with their bodies; but their heads, owing to the extreme heat of the day, were one and all ornamented with leads, or papers, or dozens of little braids, to issue later in every sort of curl known to the girl of that period. Rolling the hair on leads or papers was a favorite method of attaining the desired result, and though it often entailed a sleepless night, there were those who gladly paid the price. Others, in whose veins the blood of martyrs did not flow, substituted rags for leads and pretended that they made a more natural and less woolly curl. Heat, however, will melt the proudest head and reduce to fiddling strings the finest product of the waving-pin; so anxious mothers were stationed over their offspring, waving palm-leaf fans, it having been decided that the supreme instant when the town clock struck ten should be the one chosen for releasing the prisoners from their self-imposed tortures.

Dotted or plain Swiss muslin was the favorite garb, though there were those who were steaming in white cashmere or alpaca, because in some cases such frocks were thought more useful afterwards. Blue and pink waist ribbons were lying over the backs of chairs, and the girl who had a Roman sash was praying that she might be kept from vanity and pride.

The way to any graduating dress at all had not seemed clear to Rebecca until a month before. Then, in company with Emma Jane, she visited the Perkins attic, found piece after piece of white butter-muslin or cheesecloth, and decided that, at a pinch, it would do. The "rich blacksmith's daughter" cast the thought of dotted Swiss behind her, and elected to follow Rebecca in cheesecloth as she had in higher matters; straightway devising costumes that included such drawing of threads, such hem-stitching and pin-tucking, such insertions of fine thread tatting that, in order to be finished, Rebecca's dress was given out in sections,—the sash to Hannah, waist and sleeves to Mrs. Cobb, and skirt to Aunt Jane. The stitches that went into the despised material, worth only three or four pennies a yard, made the dresses altogether lovely, and as for the folds and lines into which they fell, they could have given points to satins and brocades.

The girls were waiting in their room alone, Emma Jane in rather a tearful state of mind. She kept thinking that it was the last day that they would be together in this altogether sweet and close intimacy. The beginning of the end seemed to have dawned, for two positions had been offered Rebecca by Mr. Morrison the day before: one in which she would play for singing and calisthenics, and superintend the piano practice of the younger girls in a boarding-school; the other an assistant's place in the Edgewood High School. Both were very modest as to salary, but the former included educational advantages that Miss Maxwell thought might be valuable.

Rebecca's mood had passed from that of excitement into a sort of exaltation, and when the first bell rang through the corridors announcing that in five minutes the class would proceed in a body to the church for the exercises, she stood motionless and speechless at the window with her hand on her heart.

"It is coming, Emmie," she said presently; "do you remember in 'The Mill on the Floss,' when Maggie Tulliver closed the golden gates of childhood behind her? I can almost see them swing; almost hear them clang; and I can't tell whether I am glad or sorry."

"I shouldn't care how they swung or clanged," said Emma Jane, "if only you and I were on the same side of the gate; but we shan't be, I know we shan't!"

"Emmie, don't dare to cry, for I'm just on the brink myself! If only you were graduating with me; that's my only sorrow! There! I hear the rumble of the wheels! People will be seeing our grand surprise now! Hug me once for luck, dear Emmie; a careful hug, remembering our butter-muslin frailty!"

Ten minutes later, Adam Ladd, who had just arrived from Portland and was wending his way to the church, came suddenly into the main street and stopped short under a tree by the wayside, riveted to the spot by a scene of picturesque loveliness such as his eyes had seldom witnessed before. The class of which Rebecca was president was not likely to follow accepted customs. Instead of marching two by two from the seminary to the church, they had elected to proceed thither by royal chariot. A haycart had been decked with green vines and bunches of long-stemmed field daisies, those gay darlings of New England meadows. Every inch of the rail, the body, even the spokes, all were twined with yellow and green and white. There were two white horses, flower-trimmed reins, and in the floral bower, seated on maple boughs, were the twelve girls of the class, while the ten boys marched on either side of the vehicle, wearing buttonhole bouquets of daisies, the class flower.

Rebecca drove, seated on a green-covered bench that looked not unlike a throne. No girl clad in white muslin, no happy girl of seventeen, is plain; and the twelve little country maids, from the vantage ground of their setting, looked beautiful, as the June sunlight filtered down on their uncovered heads, showing their bright eyes, their fresh cheeks, their smiles, and their dimples.

Rebecca, Adam thought, as he took off his hat and saluted the pretty panorama,—Rebecca, with her tall slenderness, her thoughtful brow, the fire of young joy in her face, her fillet of dark braided hair, might have been a young Muse or Sibyl; and the flowery hayrack, with its freight of blooming girlhood, might have been painted as an allegorical picture of "The Morning of Life." It all passed him, as he stood under the elms in the old village street where his mother had walked half a century ago, and he was turning with the crowd towards the church when he heard a little sob. Behind a hedge in the garden near where he was standing was a forlorn person in white, whose neat nose, chestnut hair, and blue eyes he seemed to know. He stepped inside the gate and said, "What's wrong, Miss Emma?"

"Oh, is it you, Mr. Ladd? Rebecca wouldn't let me cry for fear of spoiling my looks, but I must have just one chance before I go in. I can be as homely as I like, after all, for I only have to sing with the school; I'm not graduating, I'm just leaving! Not that I mind that; it's only being separated from Rebecca that I never can stand!"

The two walked along together, Adam comforting the disconsolate Emma Jane, until they reached the old meeting-house where the Commencement exercises were always held.

Rebecca saw Hannah and her husband in the audience; dear old John and Cousin Ann also, and felt a pang at the absence of her mother, though she had known there was no possibility of seeing her; for poor Aurelia was kept at Sunnybrook by cares of children and farm, and lack of money either for the journey or for suitable dress. The Cobbs she saw too but where was Aunt Jane, in her black silk made over especially for this occasion? Aunt Miranda had not intended to come, she knew, but where, on this day of days, was her beloved Aunt Jane? However, this thought, like all others, came and went in a flash, for the whole morning was like a series of magic-lantern pictures, crossing and recrossing her field of vision. She played, she sang, she recited Queen Mary's Latin prayer, like one in a dream, only brought to consciousness by meeting Mr. Aladdin's eyes as she spoke the last line. Then at the end of the programme came her class poem, "Makers of To-morrow"; and there, as on many a former occasion, her personality played so great a part that she seemed to be uttering Miltonic sentiments instead of school-girl verse. Her voice, her eyes, her body breathed conviction, earnestness, and emotion; and when she left the platform the audience felt that they had listened to a masterpiece. Most of her hearers knew little of

Carlyle or Emerson, or they might have remembered that the one said, "We are all poets when we read a poem well," and the other, " 'Tis the good reader makes the good book."

It was over! The diplomas had been presented, and each girl, after giving furtive touches to her hair, sly tweaks to her muslin skirts, and caressing pats to her sash, had gone forward to receive the roll of parchment with a bow that had been the subject of anxious thought for weeks. Rounds of applause greeted each graduate at this thrilling moment, and Jeremiah Cobb's behavior, when Rebecca came forward, was the talk of Wareham and Riverboro for days. Old Mrs. Webb avowed that he, in the space of two hours, had worn out her pew more—the carpet, the cushions, and woodwork—than she had by sitting in it forty years. Yes, it was over, and after the crowd had thinned a little, Adam Ladd made his way to the platform.

Rebecca turned from speaking to some strangers and met him in the aisle. "Oh, Mr. Aladdin, I am so glad you could come! Tell me"—and she looked at him half shyly, for his approval was dearer to her, and more difficult to win, than that of the others—"tell me, Mr. Aladdin,—were you satisfied?"

"More than satisfied!" he said; "glad I met the child, proud I know the girl, longing to meet the woman!"

Chapter Twenty-Four

"Th' Inevitable Yoke"

Rebecca's heart beat high at this sweet praise from her hero's lips, but before she had found words to thank him, Mr. and Mrs. Cobb, who had been modestly biding their time in a corner, approached her and she introduced them to Mr. Ladd.

"Where, where is Aunt Jane?" she cried, holding Aunt Sarah's hand on one side and Uncle Jerry's on the other.

"I'm sorry, lovey, but we've got bad news for you."

"Is Aunt Miranda worse? She is; I can see it by your looks." And Rebecca's color faded.

"She had a second stroke yesterday morning jest when she was helpin' Jane lay out her things to come here to-day. Jane said you wa'n't to know anything about it till the exercises·was all over, and we promised to keep it secret till then."

"I will go right home with you, Aunt Sarah. I must just run to tell Miss Maxwell, for after I had packed up to-morrow I was going to Brunswick with her. Poor Aunt Miranda!

And I have been so gay and happy all day, except that I was longing for mother and Aunt Jane."

"There ain't no harm in bein' gay, lovey; that's what Jane wanted you to be. And Miranda's got her speech back, for your aunt has just sent a letter sayin' she's better; and I'm goin' to set up to-night, so you can stay here and have a good sleep, and get your things together comfortably to-morrow."

"I'll pack your trunk for you, Becky dear, and attend to all our room things," said Emma Jane, who had come to-wards the group and heard the sorrowful news from the brick house.

They moved into one of the quiet side pews, where Hannah and her husband and John joined them. From time to time some straggling acquaintance or old schoolmate would come up to congratulate Rebecca and ask why she had hidden herself in a corner. Then some member of the class would call to her excitedly, reminding her not to be late at the picnic luncheon, or begging her to be early at the class party in the evening. All this had an air of unreality to Rebecca. In the midst of the happy excitement of the last two days, when "blushing honors" had been falling thick upon her, and behind the delicious exaltation of the morning, had been the feeling that the condition was a transient one, and that the burden, the struggle, the anxiety, would soon loom again on the horizon. She longed to steal away into the woods with dear old John, grown so manly and handsome, and get some comfort from him.

Meantime Adam Ladd and Mr. Cobb had been having an animated conversation.

"I s'pose up to Boston, girls like that one are as thick as blackb'ries?" Uncle Jerry said, jerking his head interrogatively in Rebecca's direction.

"They may be," smiled Adam, taking in the old man's mood; "only I don't happen to know one."

"My eyesight bein' poor's the reason she looked han'somest of any girl on the platform, I s'pose?"

"There's no failure in my eyes," responded Adam, "but that was how the thing seemed to me!"

"What did you think of her voice? Anything extry about it?"

"Made the others sound poor and thin, I thought."

"Well, I'm glad to hear your opinion, you bein' a traveled man, for mother says I'm foolish 'bout Rebecky and hev been sence the fust. Mother scolds me for spoilin' her, but I notice mother ain't fur behind when it comes to spoilin'. Land! It made me sick, thinkin' o' them parents travelin' miles to see their young ones graduate, and then when they got here hevin' to compare 'em with Rebecky. Good-bye, Mr. Ladd, drop in some day when you come to Riverboro."

"I will," said Adam, shaking the old man's hand cordially; "perhaps to-morrow if I drive Rebecca home, as I shall offer to do. Do you think Miss Sawyer's condition is serious?"

"Well, the doctor don't seem to know; but anyhow she's paralyzed, and she'll never walk fur again, poor soul! She ain't lost her speech; that'll be a comfort to her."

Adam left the church, and in crossing the common came upon Miss Maxwell doing the honors of the institution, as she passed from group to group of strangers and guests.

Knowing that she was deeply interested in all Rebecca's plans, he told her, as he drew her aside, that the girl would have to leave Wareham for Riverboro the next day.

"That is almost more than I can bear!" exclaimed Miss Maxwell, sitting down on a bench and stabbing the greensward with her parasol. "It seems to me Rebecca never has any respite. I had so many plans for her this next month in fitting her for her position, and now she will settle down to housework again, and to the nursing of that poor, sick, cross old aunt."

"If it had not been for the cross old aunt, Rebecca would still have been at Sunnybrook; and from the standpoint of educational advantages, or indeed advantages of any sort, she might as well have been in the backwoods," returned Adam.

"That is true; I was vexed when I spoke, for I thought an easier and happier day was dawning for my prodigy and pearl."

"*Our* prodigy and pearl," corrected Adam.

"Oh, yes!" she laughed. "I always forget that it pleases you to pretend you discovered Rebecca."

"I believe, though, that happier days are dawning for her," continued Adam. "It must be a secret for the present, but Mrs. Randall's farm will be bought by the new railroad. We must have right of way through the land, and the station will be built on her property. She will receive six thousand dollars, which, though not a fortune, will yield her three or four hundred dollars a year, if she will allow me to invest it for her. There is a mortgage on the land; that paid, and Rebecca self-supporting, the mother ought to push the education of the oldest boy, who is a fine, ambitious fellow. He should be taken away from farmwork and settled at his studies."

"We might form ourselves into a Randall Protective Agency, Limited," mused Miss Maxwell. "I confess I want Rebecca to have a career."

"I don't," said Adam promptly.

"Of course you don't. Men have no interest in the careers of women! But I know Rebecca better than you."

"You understand her mind better, but not necessarily her heart. You are considering her for the moment as prodigy; I am thinking of her more as pearl."

"Well," sighed Miss Maxwell whimsically, "prodigy or pearl, the Randall Protective Agency may pull Rebecca in opposite directions, but nevertheless she will follow her saint."

"That will content me," said Adam gravely.

"Particularly if the saint beckons your way." And Miss Maxwell looked up and smiled provokingly.

Rebecca did not see her Aunt Miranda till she had been at the brick house for several days. Miranda steadily refused to have any one but Jane in the room until her face had regained its natural look, but her door was always ajar, and Jane fancied she liked to hear Rebecca's quick, light step. Her mind was perfectly clear now, and, save that she could not move, she was most of the time quite free from pain, and alert in every nerve to all that was going on within or without the house. "Were the windfall apples being picked up for sauce; were the potatoes thick in the hills;

was the corn tasselin' out; were they cuttin' the upper field; were they keepin' fly-paper laid out everywheres; were there any ants in the dairy; was the kindlin' wood holdin' out; had the bank sent the cowpons?"

Poor Miranda Sawyer! Hovering on the verge of the great beyond,—her body "struck" and no longer under control of her iron will,—no divine visions floated across her tired brain; nothing but petty cares and sordid anxieties. Not all at once can the soul talk with God, be He ever so near. If the heavenly language never has been learned, quick as is the spiritual sense in seizing the facts it needs, then the poor soul must use the words and phrases it has lived on and grown into day by day. Poor Miss Miranda!— held fast within the prison walls of her own nature, blind in the presence of revelation because she had never used the spiritual eye, deaf to angelic voices because she had not used the spiritual ear.

There came a morning when she asked for Rebecca. The door was opened into the dim sick-room, and Rebecca stood there with the sunlight behind her, her hands full of sweet peas. Miranda's pale, sharp face, framed in its nightcap, looked haggard on the pillow, and her body was pitifully still under the counterpane.

"Come in," she said; "I ain't dead yet. Don't mess up the bed with them flowers, will ye?"

"Oh, no! They're going in a glass pitcher," said Rebecca, turning to the washstand as she tried to control her voice and stop the tears that sprang to her eyes.

"Let me look at ye; come closer. What dress are ye wearin'?" said the old aunt in her cracked, weak voice.

"My blue calico."

"Is your cashmere holdin' its color?"

"Yes, Aunt Miranda."

"Do you keep it in a dark closet hung on the wrong side, as I told ye?"

"Always."

"Has your mother made her jelly?"

"She hasn't said."

"She always had the knack o' writin' letters with nothin' in 'em. What's Mark broke sence I've been sick?"

"Nothing at all, Aunt Miranda."

"Why, what's the matter with him? Gittin' lazy, ain't he? How's John turnin' out?"

"He's going to be the best of us all."

"I hope you don't slight things in the kitchen because I ain't there. Do you scald the coffeepot and turn it upside down on the windersill?"

"Yes, Aunt Miranda."

"It's always 'yes' with you, and 'yes' with Jane," groaned Miranda, trying to move her stiffened body; "but all the time I lay here knowin' there's things done the way I don't like 'em."

There was a long pause, during which Rebecca sat down by the bedside and timidly touched her aunt's hand, her heart swelling with tender pity at the gaunt face and closed eyes.

"I was dreadful ashamed to have you graduate in cheese-cloth, Rebecca, but I couldn't help it nohow. You'll hear the reason some time, and know I tried to make it up to ye. I'm afraid you was a laughin'-stock!"

"No," Rebecca answered. "Ever so many people said our dresses were the very prettiest; they looked like soft lace. You're not to be anxious about anything. Here I am all grown up and graduated,—number three in a class of twenty-two, Aunt Miranda,—and good positions offered me already. Look at me, big and strong and young, all ready to go into the world and show what you and Aunt Jane have done for me. If you want me near, I'll take the Edgewood School, so that I can be here nights and Sundays to help; and if you get better, then I'll go to Augusta,—for that's a hundred dollars more, with music lessons and other things beside."

"You listen to me," said Miranda quaveringly. "Take the best place, regardless o' my sickness. I'd like to live long enough to know you'd paid off that mortgage, but I guess I shan't."

Here she ceased abruptly, having talked more than she had for weeks; and Rebecca stole out of the room, to cry by herself and wonder if old age must be so grim, so hard, so unchastened and unsweetened, as it slipped into the valley of the shadow.

The days went on, and Miranda grew stronger and stronger; her will seemed unassailable, and before long she could be moved into a chair by the window, her dominant thought being to arrive at such a condition of improvement that the doctor need not call more than once a week, instead of daily; thereby diminishing the bill, that was mounting to such a terrifying sum that it haunted her thoughts by day and dreams by night.

Little by little hope stole back into Rebecca's young

heart. Aunt Jane began to "clear-starch" her handkerchiefs and collars and purple muslin dress, so that she might be ready to go to Brunswick at any moment when the doctor pronounced Miranda well on the road to recovery. Everything beautiful was to happen in Brunswick if she could be there by August,—everything that heart could wish or imagination conceive, for she was to be Miss Emily's very own visitor, and sit at table with college professors and other great men.

At length the day dawned when the few clean, simple dresses were packed in the hair trunk, together with her beloved coral necklace, her cheesecloth graduating dress, her class pin, Aunt Jane's lace cape, and the one new hat, which she tried on every night before going to bed. It was of white chip with a wreath of cheap white roses and green leaves, and cost between two and three dollars, an unprecedented sum in Rebecca's experience. The effect of its glories when worn with her nightdress was dazzling enough, but if ever it appeared in conjunction with the cheesecloth gown, Rebecca felt that even reverend professors might regard it with respect. It is probable, indeed, that any professorial gaze lucky enough to meet a pair of dark eyes shining under that white-rose garland would never have stopped at respect!

Then, when all was ready and Abijah Flagg at the door, came a telegram from Hannah: "Come at once. Mother has had bad accident."

In less than an hour Rebecca was started on her way to Sunnybrook, her heart palpitating with fear as to what might be awaiting her at her journey's end.

Death, at all events, was not there to meet her; but something that looked at first only too much like it. Her mother had been standing on the haymow superintending some changes in the barn, had been seized with giddiness, they thought, and slipped. The right knee was fractured and the back strained and hurt, but she was conscious and in no immediate danger, so Rebecca wrote, when she had a moment to send Aunt Jane the particulars.

"I don' know how 't is," grumbled Miranda, who was not able to sit up that day; "but from a child I could never lay abed without Aurelia's gettin' sick too. I don' know's she could help fallin', though it ain't any place for a woman,—a haymow; but if it hadn't been that, 't would 'a' been somethin' else. Aurelia was born unfortunate. Now she'll probably be a cripple, and Rebecca'll have to nurse her instead of earning a good income somewheres else."

"Her first duty's to her mother," said Aunt Jane; "I hope she'll always remember that."

"Nobody remembers anything they'd ought to,—at seventeen," responded Miranda. "Now that I'm strong again, there's things I want to consider with you, Jane, things that are on my mind night and day. We've talked 'em over before; now we'll settle 'em. When I'm laid away, do you want to take Aurelia and the children down here to the brick house? There's an awful passel of 'em,—Aurelia, Jenny, and Fanny; but I won't have Mark. Hannah can take him; I won't have a great boy stompin' out the carpets and ruinin' the furniture, though I know when I'm dead I can't hinder ye, if you make up your mind to do anything."

"I shouldn't like to go against your feelings, especially in laying out your money, Miranda," said Jane.

"Don't tell Rebecca I've willed her the brick house. She won't git it till I'm gone, and I want to take my time 'bout dyin' and not be hurried off by them that's goin' to profit by it; nor I don't want to be thanked, neither. I s'pose she'll use the front stairs as common as the back and like as not have water brought into the kitchen, but mebbe when I've been dead a few years I shan't mind. She sets such store by you, she'll want you to have your home here as long's you live, but, anyway, I've wrote it down that way; though Lawyer Burns's wills don't hold more'n half the time. He's cheaper, but I guess it comes out jest the same in the end. I wa'n't goin' to have the fust man Rebecca picks up for a husband turnin' you ou'doors."

There was a long pause, during which Jane knit silently, wiping the tears from her eyes from time to time, as she looked at the pitiful figure lying weakly on the pillows. Suddenly Miranda said slowly and feebly:—

"I don' know after all but you might as well take Mark; I s'pose there's tame boys as well as wild ones. There ain't a mite o' sense in havin' so many children, but it's a turrible risk splittin' up families and farmin' 'em out here 'n' there; they'd never come to no good, an' everybody would keep rememberin' their mother was a Sawyer. Now if you'll draw down the curtin, I'll try to sleep."

Chapter Twenty-Five

Mother and Daughter

Two months had gone by,—two months of steady, fagging work; of cooking, washing, ironing; of mending and caring for the three children, although Jenny was fast becoming a notable little housewife, quick, ready, and capable. They were months in which there had been many a weary night of watching by Aurelia's bedside; of soothing and bandaging and rubbing; of reading and nursing, even of feeding and bathing. The ceaseless care was growing less now, and the family breathed more freely, for the mother's sigh of pain no longer came from the stifling bedroom, where, during a hot and humid August, Aurelia had lain, suffering with every breath she drew. There would be no question of walking for many a month to come, but blessings seemed to multiply when the blinds could be opened and the bed drawn near the window; when mother, with pillows behind her, could at least sit and watch the work going on, could smile at the past agony and forget the weary hours that had led to her present comparative ease and comfort.

No girl of seventeen can pass through such an ordeal and come out unchanged; no girl of Rebecca's temperament could go through it without some inward repining and rebellion. She was doing tasks in which she could not be fully happy,—heavy and trying tasks, which perhaps she could never do with complete success or satisfaction; and like promise of nectar to thirsty lips was the vision of joys she had had to put aside for the performance of dull daily duty. How brief, how fleeting, had been those splendid visions when the universe seemed open for her young strength to battle and triumph in! How soon they had faded into the light of common day! At first, sympathy and grief were so keen she thought of nothing but her mother's pain. No consciousness of self interposed between her and her filial service; then, as the weeks passed, little blighted hopes began to stir and ache in her breast; defeated ambitions raised their heads as if to sting her; unattainable delights teased her by their very nearness; by the narrow line of separation that lay between her and their realization. It is easy, for the moment, to tread the narrow way, looking neither to the right nor left, upborne by the sense of right doing; but that first joy of self-denial, the joy that is like fire in the blood, dies away; the path seems drearier and the footsteps falter. Such a time came to Rebecca, and her bright spirit flagged when the letter was received saying that her position in Augusta had been filled. There was a mutinous leap of the heart then, a beating of the wings against the door of the cage, a longing for the freedom of the big world outside. It was the stirring of the powers within her, though she called it by no such grand name. She felt as if the wind of destiny were blowing her flame hither and thither, burning, consuming her, but kindling nothing. All this meant one stormy night in her little room at Sunnybrook, but the clouds blew over, the sun shone again, a rainbow stretched across the sky, while "hope clad in April green" smiled into her upturned face and beckoned her on, saying:—

> Grow old along with me,
> The best is yet to be.

Threads of joy ran in and out of the gray tangled web of daily living. There was the attempt at odd moments to make the bare little house less bare by bringing in out-of-doors, taking a leaf from Nature's book and noting how she conceals ugliness wherever she finds it. Then there was the satisfaction of being mistress of the poor domain; of planning, governing, deciding; of bringing order out of chaos; of implanting gayety in the place of inert resignation to the inevitable. Another element of comfort was the children's love, for they turned to her as flowers to the sun, drawing confidently on her fund of stories, serene in the conviction that there was no limit to Rebecca's power of make-believe. In this, and in yet greater things, little as she realized it, the law of compensation was working in her behalf, for in those anxious days mother and daughter found and knew each other as never before. A new sense was born in Rebecca as she hung over her mother's bed of pain and unrest,—a sense that comes only of ministering, a sense that grows only when the strong bend toward the weak. As for Aurelia, words could never have expressed her dumb happiness when the real revelation of motherhood was vouchsafed her. In all the earlier years when her babies were young, carking cares and anxieties darkened the fireside with their brooding wings. Then Rebecca had gone away, and in the long months of absence her mind and soul had grown out of her mother's knowledge, so that now, when Aurelia had time and strength to study her child, she was like some enchanting changeling.

On a mellow October morning, Rebecca came into her mother's room, her arms full of goldenrod and flaming autumn leaves.

It was a marvelous morning. The sun had climbed into a world that held in remembrance only a succession of golden days and starlit nights. The air was fragrant with ripening fruit, and there was a mad little bird on a tree outside the door nearly bursting his throat with joy of living. He had forgotten that summer was over, that winter must ever come; and who could think of cold winds, bare boughs, or frozen streams on such a day? A painted moth came in at the open window and settled on the tuft of brilliant leaves. Aurelia heard the bird and looked from the beauty of the glowing bush to her tall, splendid daughter, standing like young Spring with golden Autumn in her arms.

Then suddenly she covered her eyes and cried, "I can't bear it! Here I lie chained to this bed, interfering with everything you want to do. It's all wasted! All my saving and doing without; all your hard study; all Mirandy's out-lay; everything that we thought was going to be the making of you!"

"Mother, mother, don't talk so, don't think so!" exclaimed Rebecca, sitting down impetuously on the floor by the bed and dropping the goldenrod by her side. "Why, Mother, I'm only a little past seventeen! This person in a purple calico apron with flour on her nose is only the beginnings of me!"

"You can put a brave face on it," sobbed Aurelia, "but you can't deceive me. You've lost your place; you'll never see your friends here, and you're nothing but a drudge!"

"I look like a drudge," said Rebecca mysteriously, with laughing eyes, "but I really am a princess; you mustn't tell, but this is only a disguise; I wear it for reasons of state."

Aurelia smiled in spite of herself, and though not perhaps wholly deceived, she was comforted.

"I only hope you won't have to wait too long for your thrones and your kingdoms, Rebecca," she said, "and that I shall have a sight of them before I die; but life looks very hard and rough to me, what with your Aunt Miranda a cripple at the brick house, me another here at the farm, you tied hand and foot, first with one and then with the other, to say nothing of Jenny and Fanny and Mark! You've got something of your father's happy disposition, or it would weigh on you as it does on me."

"Why, Mother!" cried Rebecca, clasping her knees with her hands; "why, mother, it's enough joy just to be here in the world on a day like this; to have the chance of seeing, feeling, doing, becoming! When you were seventeen, mother, wasn't it good just to be alive? You haven't forgotten?"

"No," said Aurelia, "but I wasn't so much alive as you are, never in the world."

"I often think," Rebecca continued, walking to the window and looking out at the trees,—"I often think how dreadful it would be if I were not here at all. If Hannah had come, and then, instead of me, John; John and Jenny and Fanny and the others, but no Rebecca; never any Rebecca! To be alive makes up for everything; there ought to be fears in my heart, but there aren't; something stronger sweeps them out something like a wind. Oh, see! There is Will driving up the lane, Mother, and he ought to have a letter from the brick house."

Chapter Twenty-Six

Good-bye, Sunnybrook

Will Melville drove up to the window and, tossing a letter into Rebecca's lap, went off to the barn on an errand.

"Sister's no worse, then," sighed Aurelia gratefully, "or Jane would have telegraphed. See what she says."

Rebecca opened the envelope and read in one flash of an eye the whole brief page:—

Your Aunt Miranda passed away an hour ago. Come at once, if your mother is out of danger. I shall not have the funeral till you are here. She died very suddenly and without any pain. Oh, Rebecca! I long for you so!

AUNT JANE.

The force of habit was too strong, and even in the hour of death Jane had remembered that a telegram was twenty-five cents, and that Aurelia would have to pay half a dollar for its delivery.

Rebecca burst into a passion of tears as she cried, "Poor, poor Aunt Miranda! She is gone without taking a bit of comfort in life, and I couldn't say good-bye to her! Poor lonely Aunt Jane! What can I do, mother? I feel torn in two, between you and the brick house."

"You must go this very instant," said Aurelia, starting from her pillows. "If I was to die while you were away, I would say the very same thing. Your aunts have done everything in the world for you,—more than I've ever been able to do,—and it is your turn to pay back some o' their kindness and show your gratitude. The doctor says I've turned the corner and I feel I have. Jenny can make out somehow, if Hannah'll come over once a day."

"But, mother, I *can't* go! Who'll turn you in bed?" exclaimed Rebecca, walking the floor and wringing her hands distractedly.

"It don't make any difference if I don't get turned," replied Aurelia stoically. "If a woman of my age and the mother of a family hasn't got sense enough not to slip off haymows, she'd ought to suffer. Go put on your black dress and pack your bag. I'd give a good deal if I was able to go to my sister's funeral and prove that I've forgotten and forgiven all she said when I was married. Her acts were softer'n her words, Mirandy's were, and she's made up to you for all she ever sinned against me 'n' your father! And oh, Rebecca," she continued with quivering voice, "I remember so well when we were little girls together and she took such pride in curling my hair: and another time, when we were grown up, she lent me her best blue muslin: it was when your father had asked me to lead the grand march with him at the Christmas dance, and I found out afterwards she thought he'd intended to ask her!"

Here Aurelia broke down and wept bitterly; for the recollection of the past had softened her heart and brought the comforting tears even more effectually than the news of her sister's death.

There was only an hour for preparation. Will would drive Rebecca to Temperance and send Jenny back from school. He volunteered also to engage a woman to sleep at the farm in case Mrs. Randall should be worse at any time in the night.

Rebecca flew down over the hill to get a last pail of spring water, and as she lifted the bucket from the crystal depths and looked out over the glowing beauty of the autumn landscape, she saw a company of surveyors with their instruments making calculations and laying lines that apparently crossed Sunnybrook at the favorite spot where Mirror Pool lay clear and placid, the yellow leaves on its surface no yellower than its sparkling sands.

She caught her breath. "The time has come!" she thought. "I am saying good-bye to Sunnybrook, and the golden gates that almost swung together that last day in Wareham will close forever now. Good-bye, dear brook and hills and meadows; you are going to see life too, so we must be hopeful and say to one another:—

> "Grow old along with me,
> The best is yet to be."

Will Melville had seen the surveyors too, and had heard in the Temperance post-office that morning the probable sum that Mrs. Randall would receive from the railway company. He was in good spirits at his own improved prospects, for his farm was so placed that its value could be only increased by the new road; he was also relieved in mind that his wife's family would no longer be in dire poverty directly at his doorstep, so to speak. John could now be hurried forward and forced into the position of head of the family several years sooner than had been anticipated, so Hannah's husband was obliged to exercise great self-control or he would have whistled while he was driving Rebecca to the Temperance station. He could not understand her sad face or the tears that rolled silently down her cheeks from time to time; for Hannah had always represented her Aunt Miranda as an irascible, parsimonious old woman, who would be no loss to the world whenever she should elect to disappear from it.

"Cheer up, Becky!" he said, as he left her at the station. "You'll find your mother sitting up when you come back, and the next thing you know the whole family'll be moving to some nice little house wherever your work is. Things will never be so bad again as they have been this last year; that's what Hannah and I think." And he drove away to tell his wife the news.

Adam Ladd was in the station and came up to Rebecca instantly, as she entered the door looking very unlike her bright self.

"The Princess is sad this morning," he said, taking her hand. "Aladdin must rub the magic lamp; then the slave will appear, and these tears be dried in a trice."

He spoke lightly, for he thought her trouble was something connected with affairs at Sunnybrook, and that he could soon bring the smiles by telling her that the farm was sold and that her mother was to receive a handsome price in return. He meant to remind her, too, that though she must leave the home of her youth, it was too remote a place to be a proper dwelling either for herself or for her lonely mother and the three younger children. He could hear her say as plainly as if it were yesterday, "I don't think one ever forgets the spot where one lived as a child." He could see the quaint little figure sitting on the piazza at North River-boro and watch it disappear in the lilac bushes when he gave the memorable order for three hundred cakes of Rose-Red and Snow-White soap.

A word or two soon told him that her grief was of another sort, and her mood was so absent, so sensitive and tearful, that he could only assure her of his sympathy and beg that he might come soon to the brick house to see with his own eyes how she was faring.

Adam thought, when he had put her on the train and taken his leave, that Rebecca was, in her sad dignity and gravity, more beautiful than he had ever seen her,—all-beautiful and all-womanly. He turned from the little country station to walk in the woods by the wayside until his own train should be leaving, and from time to time he threw himself under a tree to think and dream and look at the glory of the foliage. He had brought a new copy of the "Arabian Nights" for Rebecca, wishing to replace the well-worn old one that had been the delight of her girlhood; but meeting her at such an inauspicious time, he had absently carried it away with him. He turned the pages idly until he came to the story of "Aladdin and the Wonderful Lamp" and presently, in spite of his thirty-four years, the old tale held him spellbound as it did in the days when he first read it as a boy. But there were certain paragraphs that especially caught his eye and arrested his attention,—paragraphs that he read and reread, finding in them he knew not what secret delight and significance. These were the quaintly turned phrases describing the effect on the once poor Aladdin of his wonderful riches, and those descanting upon the beauty and charm of the Sultan's daughter.

Chapter Twenty-Seven

Aunt Miranda's Apology

When Rebecca alighted from the train at Maplewood and hurried to the post-office where the stage was standing, what was her joy to see Uncle Jerry Cobb holding the horses' heads.

"The reg'lar driver's sick," he explained, "and when they sent for me, thinks I to myself, my drivin' days is over, but Rebecky won't let the grass grow under her feet when she gits her Aunt Jane's letter, and like as not I'll ketch her to-day; or, if she gits delayed, to-morrow for certain. So here I be jest as I was more'n six years ago. Will you be a real lady passenger, or will ye sit up in front with me?"

Emotions of various sorts were all struggling together in the old man's face, and the two or three bystanders were astounded when they saw the handsome, stately girl fling herself on Mr. Cobb's dusty shoulder crying like a child.

"Oh, Uncle Jerry!" she sobbed; "dear Uncle Jerry! It's all so long ago, and so much has happened, and we've grown so old, and so much is going to happen that I'm fairly frightened."

"There, there, lovey," the old man whispered comfortingly, "we'll be all alone on the stage, and we'll talk things over's we go along the road an' mebbe they won't look so bad."

Every mile of the way was as familiar to Rebecca as to Uncle Jerry; every watering-trough, grindstone, red barn, weather-vane, duck-pond, and sandy brook. And all the time she was looking backward to the day, seemingly so long ago, when she sat on the box seat for the first time, her legs dangling in the air, too short to reach the footboard. She could smell the big bouquet of lilacs, see the pink-flounced parasol, feel the stiffness of the starched buff calico and the hated prick of the black and yellow porcupine quills. The drive was taken almost in silence, but it was a sweet, comforting silence both to Uncle Jerry and the girl.

Then came the sight of Abijah Flagg shelling beans in the barn, and then the Perkins attic windows with a white cloth fluttering from them. She could spell Emma Jane's loving thought and welcome in that little waving flag; a word and a message sent to her just at the first moment when River-boro chimneys rose into view; something to warm her heart till they could meet.

The brick house came next, looking just as of yore; though it seemed to Rebecca as if death should have cast some mysterious spell over it. There were the rolling meadows, the stately elms, all yellow and brown now; the glowing maples, the garden-beds bright with asters, and the hollyhocks, rising tall against the parlor windows; only in place of the cheerful pinks and reds of the nodding stalks, with their gay rosettes of bloom, was a crape scarf holding the blinds together, and another on the sitting-room side, and another on the brass knocker of the brown-painted door.

"Stop, Uncle Jerry! Don't turn in at the side; hand me my satchel, please; drop me in the road and let me run up the path by myself. Then drive away quickly."

At the noise and rumble of the approaching stage the house door opened from within, just as Rebecca closed the gate behind her. Aunt Jane came down the stone steps, a changed woman, frail and broken and white. Rebecca held out her arms and the old aunt crept into them feebly, as she did on that day when she opened the grave of her buried love and showed the dead face, just for an instant, to a child. Warmth and strength and life flowed into the aged frame from the young one.

"Rebecca," she said, raising her head, "before you go in to look at her, do you feel any bitterness over anything she ever said to you?"

Rebecca's eyes blazed reproach, almost anger, as she said chokingly: "Oh, Aunt Jane. Could you believe it of me? I am going in with a heart brimful of gratitude!"

"She was a good woman, Rebecca; she had a quick temper and a sharp tongue, but she wanted to do right, and she did it as near as she could. She never said so, but I'm sure she was sorry for every hard word she spoke to you; she didn't take 'em back in life, but she acted so't you'd know her feeling when she was gone."

"I told her before I left that she'd been the making of me, just as mother says," sobbed Rebecca.

"She wasn't that," said Jane. "God made you in the first place, and you've done considerable yourself to help Him along; but she gave you the wherewithal to work with, and that ain't to be despised; specially when anybody gives up her own luxuries and pleasures to do it. Now let me tell you something, Rebecca. Your Aunt Mirandy's willed all this to you,—the brick house and buildings and furniture, and the land all round the house, as far's you can see."

Rebecca threw off her hat and put her hand to her heart, as she always did in moments of intense excitement. After a moment's silence she said: "Let me go in alone; I want to talk to her; I want to thank her; I feel as if I could make her hear and feel and understand!"

Jane went back into the kitchen to the inexorable tasks that death has no power, even for a day, to blot from existence. He can stalk through dwelling after dwelling, leaving despair and desolation behind him, but the table must be laid, the-dishes washed, the beds made, by somebody.

Ten minutes later Rebecca came out from the Great Presence looking white and spent, but chastened and glorified. She sat in the quiet doorway, shaded from the little Riverboro world by the overhanging elms. A wide sense of thankfulness and peace possessed her, as she looked at the autumn landscape, listened to the rumble of a wagon on the bridge, and heard the call of the river as it dashed to the sea. She put up her hand softly and touched first the shining brass knocker and then the red bricks, glowing in the October sun.

It was home; her roof, her garden, her green acres, her dear trees; it was shelter for the little family at Sunnybrook; her mother would have once more the companionship of her sister and the friends of her girlhood; the children would have teachers and playmates.

And she? Her own future was close-folded still; folded and hidden in beautiful mists; but she leaned her head against the sun-warmed door, and closing her eyes, whispered, just as if she had been a child saying her prayers: "God bless Aunt Miranda; God bless the brick house that was; God bless the brick house that is to be!"